W9-BNN-410

INDIAN SUMMER

INDIAN SUMMER

Barbara Girion

**SCHOLASTIC
HARDCOVER**

Scholastic Inc.
New York

Library of Congress Cataloging-in-Publication Data

Girion, Barbara, 1937–
Indian summer / Barbara Girion.
p.   cm.
Summary: While spending summer vacation on an Indian reservation,
twelve-year-old Joni has a difficult time getting along with Sarah Birdsong
and her friends, who seem to hold her responsible for the prejudice they
experience outside the reservation.

ISBN 0-590-42636-2

1. Indians of North America — Reservations — Juvenile fiction. [1.
Indians of North America — Reservations — Fiction. 2. Prejudices —
Fiction.]   I. Title.
PZ7.G43979In   1990
[Fic] — dc20   89-10835
                                                       CIP
                                                        AC

12 11 10 9 8 7 6 5 4 3 2 1   0 1 2 3 4 5/9

Printed in the U.S.A.   37

First Scholastic printing, April 1990

*For all young Native Americans
who proudly carry on
the language, traditions, and culture
of their Indian way of life*

Acknowledgments

Although this is a work of fiction and there is no Woodland Reservation, I was lucky enough to visit the Tuscarora, Cattaraugus, and Tonawanda Reservations in New York State. The characters in *Indian Summer* are fictional, but the wonderful people I met on my trip are real. They gave me hospitality and wisdom, and I would like to thank them.

Timothy J. Toohey, Esq., of Buffalo, New York, took time from a busy law practice to help a stranger with an idea. Without his introductions, his time, and attention, I would never have known how to start. His wisdom, sense of justice, and fairness set the tone of my research.

Bliss Broyard was a witty and indefatigable research assistant who kept me organized and centered as we adventured through the reservations.

To the Murdoch family — Maureen, Clifford,

Tony Patterson, Troy and Tricia — my thanks for showing me Mother Earth, the sky, and all the beauties that the Creator wants us to watch over.

Neville and Juanita Spring shared stories and their beautiful Native American jewelry.

Ramona Charles is as wise and kind as the very trees that shelter us.

At the Iroquois Crossroads Center, Kim Hoffman gave much of her time, and Marilyn Miller acted as a guide on our day trips.

Thanks to Chris Le Beau of the Cattaraugus Health Center, Crystal Jimerson of the Seneca Nation Early Childhood Center, and new friends at the Seneca Nation Library, where I was proud to find some of my earlier published books.

And to all my new Native American friends, young and old, who took time to talk and to teach, my love and thanks.

Barbara Girion
Short Hills, N.J.
Fall 1989

INDIAN SUMMER

One

Dear Sarah Birdsong:

My name is Joni McCord and my father told
me to write because it looks like I'll be meeting
you this summer. Not just me, but my whole family!! My father is Dr. McCord — he's a pediatrician and he gives practically painless shots!! (Ha
ha.) And there's my mom. Do you like chocolate
chip cookies? She makes great ones. Almost as
good as Famous Amos's! There's my brother
Alex — he's kind of cute, I guess — the girls in
high school go crazy over him. Do you have any
brothers or sisters? (Oh, yes, Alex can be a real
pain, especially when his friends are around and
he tells me to get lost.)

Do you have any brothers or sisters? (Excuse
me, I know I asked you that already but I'm using
my father's computer and I don't know how to

delete that.) Do you have computers in school? That's where I learned (almost) to use one. Do you have any pets?

What's your favorite music? I love Madonna.

We have a mall near our house and I like to hang out with my friends when my mom lets me.

Do you have a mall where you live? If you do, I'm sure my mom will drive us — we're coming up in our station wagon.

Our town just built a pool and I was hoping to swim there this summer with my friends. Then my dad came home and told me to write you a letter because we're going to be on your reservation for a month. My dad said you might have a pool or a lake nearby where we can swim.

Please answer soon. My father said I have to write to you three times before we get to the reservation.

Joni McCord

P.S. I forgot to tell you about my brother Mikey. He's almost five. Ready for kindergarten and gets away with murder because he's the baby and so cute. I have to baby-sit a lot for him. But my mom said I won't have to watch him so much on the reservation.

Joni McCord tried to watch her father's face as he read the letter. Steven McCord had his glasses pulled to the edge of his nose, which made him look very stern. Joni kicked the edge of the desk:

4

tap, tap, tap. Uh-oh! Her father smoothed the edges of the computer paper. He was wearing his *I'm-about-to-tell-you-that-I'm-disappointed-in-you* look.

Joni blew back the bangs that fell into her eyes. She needed a haircut. Her dark brown hair fell every which way around her shoulders.

"Between your puffing and kicking that desk, you sound like a steam engine." Dr. McCord handed the letter back. "You could be a little more enthusiastic in your letter, Joni."

"What do you mean?"

"You sound as if you're being forced to go up there — "

Joni never let her father finish. The puffing stopped and she burst into tears. "But you *are* forcing me to go. I was going to have the greatest summer of my entire life. This is the first year the pool is open. Everyone's going to be there. The whole town, except me!"

"Now, Joni, we've been all through this." Joni's mother, Carol McCord, had been quiet until now. But she reached over and smoothed the bangs back from Joni's face. She always tried to ease tough situations with a touch or a kiss, but right now Joni wasn't having any of it.

Joni left the letter and her parents and ran to her room. She slammed the door and locked herself in. Well, not really, because she didn't have a lock, but she did put a chair against the door, until she realized that no one was going to break in anyway.

Just two weeks before, her summer had been set. Then her father had announced that the whole family was going to the Woodland Reservation, home of some Iroquois Indians, for a *month!* He was taking the place of his good friend Dr. Ken Gold, another pediatrician who ran a clinic there.

Carol McCord had thought it would be a great adventure, but then she always agreed with Joni's father. Mikey was too little to care, and Alex had gotten a funny look in his eyes. He was supposed to be a lifeguard at the new pool, but he didn't say anything to his father. Joni had gone crazy. She had dropped the roll she was eating straight into her tomato soup and splashed the front of one of her favorite T-shirts. A *month* — in the summer! And she was going into the sixth grade in September! That was the hardest, scariest grade. If she wasn't around all summer, everyone would forget about her.

When fathers make up their minds, there's not much you can do. Dr. McCord had all kinds of papers in his briefcase, and one of them had an address of an Indian girl the same age as Joni.

"My friend Ken thought this would be helpful, Joni. Now, dry those tears and write to this girl. Let's see. Her name is Sarah Birdsong."

"Sarah Birdsong! What kind of a name is that?" Alex asked.

Steven McCord ignored him. "We should think of this as an adventure! We'll meet new people and learn about Native Americans firsthand. Besides, it's only one month!"

There was a knock on Joni's door. She reached for her tissues and sniffed loudly. Her eyes were red and there were ridges on her cheeks from the lines in her corduroy bedspread.

"It's Mom. Open up, Joni."

Her mother had the letter in her hand. She tried to hug Joni, but Joni held herself rigid. It was too easy to let her mom smooth away all the bad things. But even if she wanted a big hug and kiss, nothing was changed. She still had to go to the reservation.

"Address the envelope and we'll put it in tomorrow's mail. Why don't you put some of your pretty stickers on the envelope?"

Because that would be too friendly, Joni wanted to say. She had a box filled with stickers, rainbows and hearts, pretty flowers, and all kinds of different animals. The stickers were for her friends, not some Indian girl that she didn't know or care about.

With her mother watching, Joni addressed the envelope and shoved the letter in. Mrs. McCord was waiting. Joni sighed and opened her sticker box. She found an ugly sticker on the bottom of a long sheet. It had a garish palm tree and a huge orange sun. "Here!" Joni pulled it off and stuck it on the back. "Finished," she said to her mother.

"Return address, Joni." Now Carol McCord was the one tapping her foot and puffing like a steam engine as she waited for Joni to finish.

Two

Dear Sarah Birdsong:

This is the second letter (number two — numero dos, as we say in our beginning Spanish class) that I've written. Do you take Spanish in school? My dad says Dr. Ken told him that we're about the same age and we'll be renting rooms in your grandmother's house. I guess you've been too busy to answer my first letter, but Dad says I have to keep writing.

Guess what? Remember I wrote you about my brother Alex? Well, he's not coming with us. It's because of the town pool. He got a job as a junior lifeguard, and he's going to live with his best friend. Isn't that lucky for him? My mom and dad had a fight about it, but Alex won.

Besides the new pool, there's a recreation area for games and things. They're going to have swim-

ming meets with trophies and barbecues and plays. All kinds of stuff. They even have a day camp for little kids, so I wouldn't have had to watch Mikey.

I asked if I could stay with my best friend, Mandy Burnett, but Daddy said no. Maybe I should try to get a lifeguard job! (Ha ha — just kidding.)

Joni McCord

P.S. Mandy is in my room waiting for me to finish this letter. She said to ask if you have lots of that pretty silver jewelry with turquoise that we always see Indians wearing. Maybe, if it doesn't cost too much, I can bring her back a present. Petey Mann (he's also going into the sixth grade) heard I was going to a reservation this summer, and wants to know if you do rain dances and stuff like we see in the movies.

I'm going to bring my new Walkman. Dad says I can have two new tapes, because I'm being such a good sport about leaving all my friends. If you have some tapes, maybe we can trade.

Have to go now. Oh, did I tell you my mom's a librarian? She said she's going to help with your reservation library. The town paper also asked her to keep a diary of our adventures. She's supposed to mail an article every week to be published. Petey Mann says maybe she can send it by smoke signals. (Ha ha!)

Joni McCord

Amanda Burnett had come by to give Joni a going-away present. It was a little box of stationery: soft pink paper with rosebuds on the corners. "I know you won't have your dad's computer on the reservation, so I thought you might use this to write on."

"Oh, thanks, Mandy. I'll probably write you every single day. Maybe twice a day. What else will I be able to do up there?"

"Where did you say this reservation place was again?"

"My dad says up in New York State, all the way near Canada."

"That's funny, I thought all the Indians were out West. You know, with the cowboys, like the movies."

"Not all of them. Anyway, these are the Thanksgiving Indians, the ones who met the Pilgrims."

"Well, you never know. Maybe it'll be fun."

Fun! Sure, it was easy for Mandy to say. She wasn't the one who had to go. Mandy stood up and stretched. "I have to go now. So your father will bring you over tonight for supper, right?"

"Right," Joni answered. She knew there was a surprise going-away party for her at Mandy's house. At least it was a surprise until Petey Mann let it slip.

It started out wonderfully. Mandy's mother had made colored cupcakes with *GOOD LUCK, JONI* written in white icing. Joni felt a little embarrassed about being the guest of honor. Most of the kids there didn't care that she was going away, they were just happy there was a party.

Petey Mann was the one who started the Indian jokes. He pulled the back of her hair and shouted, "Way to go, Pocahontas." Joni bit her lower lip. Her stomach started to flutter the way it did when she ate too many M & M's. Why did I ever imagine he was cute? she thought.

But then Mandy, her best friend in the whole world, laughed and said she hoped Joni would come home with her scalp on. Mrs. Burnett brought out some paper napkins and said she thought the whole McCord family was "brave" to be going to a reservation. But Joni didn't think Mrs. Burnett thought the family was brave at all. It sounded to her as if Mrs. Burnett thought the whole family was crazy.

Then Petey asked if the McCords were going to live in a teepee and smoke peace pipes. Joni couldn't take any more. All the fights with her parents, the letters she had been forced to write, and now Petey's teasing were too much. She reached out and punched him in the ribs. Petey was holding a glass of bright pink Kool-Aid. When Joni's punch landed, his hand shook, and he spilled the drink all over the back of Mandy's new white sweater. Mandy cried and ran upstairs to change her clothes. Courtney told Joni she was already acting like a perfect "savage." When Mandy came back to the party, all the girls followed her to the other side of the room and started dancing together. Petey took the boys to the opposite corner, where they threw popcorn at each other. Joni sat alone in the middle of the room, played with her sneaker laces, and pretended she didn't care about any of them.

By the time Dr. McCord came to pick Joni up, hardly anyone bothered to say good-bye, except for Mrs. Burnett. Joni was quiet in the car, and her eyes were filled with tears. If she talked, she was afraid the tears would spill out. Well, that was that. She might as well stay on the Indian reservation for the rest of her life. She was sure that the kids, all the popular ones anyway, wouldn't be her friends anymore no matter *when* she came home!

Three

In a small wooden frame house nestled in the trees on Woodland Reservation, another young girl stood with eyes filled with tears. Sarah Birdsong was about the same size as Joni McCord. She wore her hair in bangs also, dark shiny black hair that hung down to her shoulders. Her black eyes were snapping as she read the letters from Joni.

"I hate it. I hate it. Another do-gooder is coming. Dr. Ken is going on vacation and some doctor from New Jersey is taking his place. And he's bringing his daughter and his son."

Sarah's grandmother stood silently scrubbing down an old porcelain sink that shone dark gray where it had been worn bare. "I knew the family would be coming. You forget your pa is chief. He had to give his permission."

14

"Why doesn't anybody tell *me*? Why do they have to stay at *our* house?"

"Dr. Ken's apartment is outside the reservation and too small for the whole family."

"That's what I mean, Maw Maw." Sarah turned pleading eyes to her grandmother. "Why does this doctor have to bring his whole family? Am I expected to spend a month baby-sitting his daughter?"

"She's the same age you are. It would be nice if you could be friends."

"Then Pa will be all upset. You know how he feels when white people don't understand reservation life or our history."

"It will be our job to help them understand."

"Since Dr. Ken asked me to, I'll write her. But remember the last white visitors that were here? They expected us to play tom-toms all day, swallow live rattlesnakes, walk barefoot over hot coals, and do rain dances."

Sarah's grandmother, Rachel Birdsong, put her hand into a pottery bowl that was loaded with odds and ends. "Here," she said, handing Sarah a ball-point pen that read SOUVENIR OF NIAGARA FALLS. "Write the letter."

"Maybe I can stay next door in the trailer with Pa, Maw Maw."

Now it was Rachel Birdsong's eyes that flashed. "No! You will stay here in the house with me. This is your home."

It was an all-wood house that had been built by Sarah's father, Chief David Birdsong. It was small and the rooms were on one floor except for the attic loft where Sarah slept. All the woodworking had been done with care. There were special carvings around the door and windowsills. All the Birdsongs had lived together until Sarah's mother had decided to leave the reservation.

When Carlenia Birdsong left, Sarah's pa moved out also. He stayed next door in an old trailer that was practically falling apart. He ate most of his meals with Sarah and her Maw Maw, but the bedroom he had shared with Sarah's mother was still and empty.

Dear Joni McCord:
I got both of your letters. The government of the United States has a small post office outside our lands. We have our own government on the Woodland Reservation. My pa is chief, Chief David Birdsong. We're part of the Iroquois Confederacy. Dr. Ken has told us about your family. We don't have a mall on the reservation. We don't have a pool, either. But we Indians prefer our lake that's filled with pure water from the snow on the mountains. It also has an underground stream that feeds into it. That's where me and my friends swim. But you have to be a good swimmer because there's no shallow parts to walk through. So far, the lake isn't polluted from the white man's fac-

16

tories. *My pa, along with chiefs from other reservations, is fighting the government because they want to put a dam up and take away some of our land.*

Some people have a satellite dish to get a clear TV picture. We don't because we don't even have a TV. The nearest mall is about sixty miles away. Maybe your dad would rather have you stay there? There's a hotel and swimming pool. They even have a baby pool to wade in. Then he could visit you on the weekends.

Sarah Birdsong

P.S. I go to a magnet school right outside the reservation. It specializes in Indian history. At the end of the year we had an exhibition on tomahawks that were used for scalping early settlers. You can still see some dried blood on the edges.

P.P.S. Why would we learn Spanish in our school? We have our own language. We also have our own music. Songs that Madonna doesn't know.

Sarah smiled as she finished the letter. Her Maw Maw watched her closely. "That wasn't so bad, was it?"

She hated to fool Maw Maw, and most of the time she couldn't hide from those faded black eyes. Maw Maw was like a laser beam that could see right through your skin and bones and read all your most secret thoughts. Sarah quickly folded the letter and sealed the envelope. When Maw Maw left the room, Sarah pricked her finger with the sharp end of an opened paper clip.

"Ouch." She smeared some blood on the back of the envelope and wrote in big letters: *S.W.B.A.G.!* There, let that little white girl from New Jersey figure that out!

Four

Joni was on the portable phone, reading Sarah's letter to Mandy. As soon as the Kool-Aid stains had washed out of Mandy's sweater, the girls had made up.

"What do you think 'S.W.B.A.G.' means?" Joni asked.

"Well, 'S.W.A.K.' means 'Sealed With a Kiss,' " said Mandy.

"I know that. So maybe the first letters mean 'Sealed With' . . . but what about the rest?"

"I don't know. You said the back of the envelope is colored?"

"Yes, it looks like red ink that got wet and smeared."

"Red?" Mandy asked.

"Red."

"Well, Joni, maybe it's blood."

"Blood!"

"Could be. After all, they *are* Indians." Mandy's voice got very low. "Why doesn't your father go up alone? Isn't your mom scared? Aren't you scared?"

There was no sense in telling Mandy how many fights Joni had lost with Dr. McCord over this trip. She fingered the back of the envelope again. " 'S.W.B.A.G.' 'Sealed With Blood' . . . maybe, but what about the other two letters?"

"You've got me. You have to write another letter, don't you? So ask her. Boy, I'd die if I was going up there."

Joni sighed as she hung up the phone. Should she write this letter on the computer or use the pretty paper that Mandy had given her? She flopped on her bed. Her mother had just redone the room in honor of Joni's going into the sixth grade. All the pink and white ruffles were gone. There was a plaid corduroy spread on the bed, and matching drapes on the windows. The soft green carpeting picked up one of the colors in the plaid, and felt warm and fluffy when Joni got out of bed in the morning. She had a desk and an open book-case that held her stereo, records, and a small TV that Grandma McCord didn't use anymore. There were big leather pillows on the floor for her friends to sit on when they came to visit. Most of her dolls and stuffed animals had been put away. An al-most-sixth-grader was too old for dolls. But her favorite Raggedy Ann, which was missing one button eye and had no shoes, still sat on her bed. Sometimes even an almost-sixth-grader needed something familiar to hug.

Joni would really miss her room this summer. Actually she would miss the whole house. She wondered if they had air-conditioning on the reservation. Sometimes Mikey's allergies acted up when it was hot, and he'd sneeze and keep everyone up all night if there was no air-conditioning.

Joni decided to use the new stationery.

Dear Sarah Birdsong:
Only a week left before we'll be on the reservation. My father has lots of special medical supplies that he's ordered.

Joni chewed on the tip of her pen. She took it out of her mouth and read the writing on the pen: *SOUVENIR OF DISNEY WORLD.* Boy, that had been a great family trip.

Our family went to Disney World this year. Have you ever been there? We flew and everything. It was the fourth time I've been on an airplane.
I told my best friend, Mandy, about your letter and we were trying to figure out what S.W.B.A.G. means. Could you please tell me when you write

21

back? We've tried all combinations but can't figure it out.

I guess your father must be pretty important if he's a chief. Does he wear those big headdresses of feathers like we see in the movies?

Joni McCord

P.S. Is your TV broken? It sounded in your letter like you don't have TV at all. My friend Petey Mann says that's impossible. Everybody has TV.

Sarah Birdsong tore Joni's latest letter in half, then in half again and again, until there was nothing left but small pink dots like confetti. She leaned out of her window and watched the pieces drift slowly to the ground like a tiny pink snow flurry.

What could she say to keep this Joni person from coming up there? Chief Birdsong was already getting upset. At dinner he had rattled the dishes when he slammed his hand against the wooden table. "Why don't we have our own Indian boys coming back here as doctors?"

Maw Maw tried to soothe him. "It takes time. Education is the answer. We have to educate more of our young people."

This was an old argument. Sarah practically knew it by heart.

"But as soon as our young people get educated, they leave and go out into the white world."

Sarah held her breath; she knew what he was

thinking because she was thinking it, too. Her father didn't say it, but he meant Carlenia Birdsong, his wife and Sarah's mother. She had left them behind to go out into the white world.

No, she wouldn't think about that now. She reached for her Niagara Falls pen. That had been a nice family trip. Pa, Maw Maw, and of course, Mom. They had driven in an old pickup truck. Sarah and Mom had sat in the back and it had been so much fun. The sun had shone brightly on their faces, but the speed of the truck caused a nice breeze. They had had a picnic lunch at the edge of the falls, and Maw Maw had told the old Indian legend about a giant snake that was killed by thunderbolts because it was poisoning the springs in a village. The great dead snake was so enormous that when they threw it in the Niagara River it got stuck on the rocks, and the weight formed the curving cliffs around the falls. If you squinted your eyes through all the mist the water made, you could actually see the shape of the snake. Sarah had shivered, and her mother had given her a big hug as she pointed to the coils around the great falls.

Dear Joni McCord:
S.W.B.A.G. means 'Sealed With Blood And Guts!' You must know how bloodthirsty we Indians are from all the movies you watch. Sure, my father has a special headdress. It was handed

down from chiefs who went before him. He keeps it on the wall next to his bow and arrow and his spears.

My best friend's name is Canada Shenandoah. She was named that because she was born right over the border in Canada, and her mother came from the Shenandoah Valley.

In one of your letters you asked me about pets. I don't have any in particular. But the whole forest is filled with animals that are my pets. Do you like rabbits? My Maw Maw (grandmother) makes great rabbit stew. Or maybe you'd like dog stew? Don't those stupid movies you watch tell you that all Indians eat dog meat?

Sarah Birdsong

P.S. Tell your friends that every year people — visitors, especially — disappear. Sometimes their bodies are found after the snow melts or when we drag the river.

Five

Joni read the last part of Sarah Birdsong's letter over and over. She shivered every time she read about people disappearing. And dog meat stew? Mom had said she was sure Sarah had been joking. Daddy agreed. "It sounds like both of you girls are trying hard not to be friendly before you even meet."

Joni didn't think that was fair. She had written great letters. She had asked a lot of questions, but so what? This was supposed to be a great adventure, a time to learn about new things. How could you learn if you didn't ask questions?

The McCords were finally on their way. Joni was crunched in the backseat of the overstuffed station wagon. There were cardboard boxes with sharp edges that stuck her in the ribs every time the car hit a bump.

Joni's mom had cried when they said good-bye to Alex. Joni had almost felt sad until he had said, "Hey, bring me back some wampum, little sister."

At the last minute Joni had run up to her room to give one last look around and say good-bye. She smoothed the pillows on her bed and her hands patted the skirts of Raggedy Ann. She hesitated, then grabbed her old friend and playmate. Maybe the Indian girl would think it was babyish. Well, she wasn't going to sleep with it. She would use the doll on her bed on the reservation as a decoration. Just like she used it here.

They had been driving for hours and hours. Mikey was being a pain. He was in the front seat, lying in Mrs. McCord's lap, dizzy from counting blue cars. They had all tried to keep him from being bored. Joni was feeling a little dizzy also, but maybe it was from the box of Fig Newtons she had practically finished herself.

They had just passed through Buffalo, New York. Steven McCord said a lot of the Indians worked in Buffalo and then went home on the weekends to the reservation. "How far, Daddy?" she asked.

"Almost there, honey." Dr. McCord had been saying "almost there" for the last fifty miles or so.

"Isn't it gorgeous up here?" Mrs. McCord said, pointing out the window. "Look at the trees and over there — see the sun sparkling on the water?"

Joni didn't think the trees looked any different from the trees in New Jersey. Neither did the water. "New Jersey is called the Garden State, Mom."

"I know. It just seems as if the air smells fresher here."

"Yes," added Joni. "As fresh as the letters from Sarah Birdsong."

Dr. McCord rubbed the back of his neck. "I've told you that your letters were not exactly friendly, either."

"Aren't we there yet?" asked Mikey.

"Almost, hon," Dr. McCord said.

"You've been telling me 'almost' for a long time," Mikey whined.

Mrs. McCord straightened her shoulders. "Steve, are you sure we didn't miss a turn?"

"Positive. I've followed the directions. We left the state highway at exit 105 and — "

"Stop, Dad. . . . There!" Joni yelled at her father. She turned around in her seat. "I saw a sign for the entrance to the reservation back there."

Dr. McCord stepped on the brakes and backed up the car slowly.

Mikey jumped up and down in the front seat. "We're here! We're here!"

"Shh . . . Hang on, Mikey, and let Daddy see where he's going."

"There." Joni tapped on the window and

27

pointed to a sign. It was almost overgrown with vines and was so small that it was easy to overlook. The letters were faded but there it was. "Wood-land Reservation."

"Good eyes, Joni. Glad you were alert. It's starting to get dark." Dr. McCord steered the station wagon onto the narrow, rough reservation road. Joni shivered. It was as if they had entered a strange country.

She had taken out Raggedy Ann from the plastic shopping bag she had stuffed her in. Just to make sure she didn't wrinkle. But now she was glad she had something to hang on to. Besides, Raggedy Ann smelled like home.

"Ouch!" Again the boxes jabbed Joni in the side as the car hit a huge bump in the road. "I'm going to have a black-and-blue tattoo on my side from these boxes," she said.

Mikey started to jump again. "Wow, ride 'em cowboy." He whooped as the car bounced and bumped along the narrow, unpaved road.

"What happened to the road, Steve? There's no pavement, just dirt and crushed rocks," Carol McCord said.

"Reservation land," answered Dr. McCord. "I don't think they get the same attention as the regular state properties."

The streetlights had been left behind when they entered the reservation, and it was getting darker by the minute. Without lights the huge trees, evergreens and maples, looked like monsters with creepy arms that met across the road.

There was a blast of loud country music. "Steven!" Mrs. McCord yelled. A large pickup truck came around a curve in the road and was driving straight toward the station wagon.

"Hold tight, everyone!" Dr. McCord swerved off the road and slammed on the brakes. The front tires had just missed a huge ditch in the side of the road. It was lucky that no one got hurt.

The pickup never stopped. Joni could see that the open back was filled with teenagers. They whooped and hollered as they passed the stalled station wagon. Beer and soda cans hit the side of the car roof.

Dr. McCord reached over and rubbed the back of Mrs. McCord's neck. The only sound was the faint music that was still coming from the speeding pickup. Even Mikey was quiet.

"Whew!" Dr. McCord let out a deep breath. "Teenagers are teenagers no matter where they are."

"They could have caused a terrible accident," said Mrs. McCord.

"At least they were playing cool music," Mikey added.

Joni didn't say a word. Her father was right; these kids were just like the group from Millburn High School who rode around town liked they owned the place.

"Looks like they're gone. Shall we move on?" Dr. McCord took out the written instructions again. "Let's see what we look for next." He and Mrs. McCord hunched over the dashboard light, studying the paper.

Joni suddenly wished she didn't have the best eyes in the car. Her heart was going at double speed, and she practically squeezed Raggedy Ann in half. Out of the dark night, three huge men dressed in jeans and plaid work shirts appeared. Joni could see the moonlight reflecting off their large silver belt buckles. They hadn't been there a minute before. Their hands were folded across their chests. The tree branches threw shadows across their faces, so it was impossible to tell whether or not they were smiling.

"Daddy! Mom!"

"What's the matter?" They turned to look at Joni. She pointed to the front of the car.

It was quiet for another moment. Then Mikey bounced up in his seat and, pointing his fingers like a gun, scrunched up his eyes and aimed. "Bang. Bang. I think we found the Indians, Daddy."

Six

Sarah Birdsong's words came back to Joni. The business about visitors disappearing, never to be seen again. Joni knew her father could handle most situations. She had seen him quiet a baby while putting stitches in its tiny head and had watched him set broken bones with his bare hands. But the McCords were miles from home on a dark road in a strange place. The three big men in front of the car didn't look as if they needed any stitches.

The tallest man stepped over to Joni's father's window. "Dr. McCord?"

"Yes, that's me." Dr. McCord rolled his window down some more and shook hands with the huge man.

"I'm David Birdsong. We've spoken on the phone."

31

"How did you know it was my daddy?" yelled Mikey, still pointing his index fingers as if they were guns.

"We know all the regular cars on the reservation. Not too many strangers wander off the main road, so we were pretty sure it was you."

Joni tried to catch her breath. So this was Sarah 's father, the chief. Well, he seemed friendly enough. It was silly to be scared. Maybe she had seen too many cowboy and Indian movies. It was just so dark. There were only tiny pinpoints of lights coming through the trees. Maybe they were from houses; she couldn't be sure. Joni couldn't remember being in a place that didn't have streetlights to help you see at night.

There were a lot of barking and howling noises in the air. Right through the darkness. Just like a mystery program.

It almost seemed as if Chief Birdsong could read her mind. "Dogs," he said. "We have lots of stray dogs. Our people leave food out for them."

Joni almost gagged. The dog stew. No, that was silly. The chief didn't say they *ate* them. He said they left food out and took care of stray dogs.

"Don't worry, Mrs. McCord. The dogs don't bother anyone unless they get teased."

Great, thought Joni. Maybe they don't eat them, but they've got packs of wild dogs around.

"Bang," said Mikey again. "Don't worry, Mom. I'll protect you from any wild animals."

Joni grimaced. Our family needs protection from Mikey and his mouth, she thought. Usually everyone that met Mikey thought he was adorable. Because he was little and cute, he got away with saying anything that came into his mind. But these men weren't smiling.

"You won't need your guns up here, son," said Chief Birdsong, who gently reached through the car window and covered Mikey's fingers with his own. "Remember, on the reservation, the Indians are the good guys and you're the ones who are different."

Dr. and Mrs. McCord laughed, but it didn't sound like a joke to Joni. It sounded more like a warning.

Nothing stopped Mikey. "If you're the chief, how come you don't have your feathers on?"

This time all the men laughed. "Only when we go on the warpath, Mikey."

Chief Birdsong told Dr. McCord to follow the bend in the road and where to make his turn. The men would cut across the fields and meet them at the Birdsong house.

Dr. McCord drove slowly around the curving road. Joni pressed her nose against the window, trying to see what the reservation looked like. The moon went in and out, and other than the headlights there were no other lights to help her see. She saw lots of trees and bushes. The houses must be set back, she thought, because you couldn't see them from the road. There were no stores — not even a gas station.

At the final turn there was a driveway to the left. There were bright porch lights, and a large older woman was standing by an open front door.

"This is my mother, Rachel Birdsong." Chief Birdsong turned to Joni. "You'll meet Sarah in a little while."

Joni jumped as the car door slammed. The men had started to unpack the car. They must have been excellent hunters because they moved so quietly. They balanced the boxes and suitcases from the station wagon as if they were kindergarten building blocks.

"Come in, come in. And I would be pleased if you would all call me Maw Maw." Maw Maw opened the door wider and shook hands with Dr. and Mrs. McCord. She stood straight and tall, and her hair was wrapped in braids piled like a crown around the top of her head. Rachel Birdsong wasn't just Sarah's Maw Maw. She was a Clan Mother to the people on the reservation. This was an honor given to the wisest women who knew everything about the history of their people. The Clan Mother was also the one who nominated the chief and kept watch that he did his job well.

Mikey looked around the house. "This doesn't look like an igloo!" he said.

Mrs. McCord was very embarrassed, and she gave Mikey a gentle poke in the shoulder. "Eskimos in Alaska live in igloos, Mikey, not Indians. I mean, not Native Americans."

Joni knew what Mikey had meant even though she would never say anything about it out loud. Here they were in a plain wooden house. Even though it was small, it could have been in New Jersey or California or Ohio. Remembering how her friends had teased her, Joni had half expected to find herself in a teepee with a fire in the middle.

She wouldn't even be able to write Mandy a letter about sleeping on branches or pillows stuffed with leaves, because there was an old but clean couch with a brightly colored Indian blanket thrown over it. Some adventure, she thought! For this she had lost the chance to spend the summer with the most popular kids in the sixth grade.

Her body felt cramped and stiff from sitting in the car for so long. The house seemed small with all the people in it. She wondered where Sarah was. She couldn't have been too anxious to meet the people who were coming to stay in her house.

Maw Maw took charge. "Let's just leave the boxes and suitcases. You all look very tired. Let me get you settled and we'll learn about each other tomorrow."

"I'm hungry," said Mikey.

"Mikey!" Mrs. McCord had that embarrassed pinch in her voice again.

"I expected you to be hungry, riding in a car for so many hours. I made sandwiches because I

35

wasn't sure what time you would be arriving."

Maw Maw pointed to a doorway in the corner. "There's the bathroom. I'll show you where you're going to sleep."

Mikey opened the bathroom door. "It *is* a bathroom," he said. "My brother Alex told me we'd have to go to an outhouse, and there'd be snakes and bats and we'd have to use pieces of newspaper instead of — "

This time Dr. McCord was the embarrassed one. He reached over and covered Mikey's mouth gently with his hand. "That's enough, Mikey." He spoke directly to the chief and Maw Maw. "My oldest son is a big teaser."

"There are lots of families on the reservation that still have to use an outhouse and have no electricity or running water." Maw Maw put her arm around Mikey and led him to a large wooden kitchen table. "But you'll have time to learn all about us."

Mikey kind of relaxed and leaned against Maw Maw. Dr. and Mrs. McCord gave grateful sighs.

There was a huge platter of sandwiches. As Joni ate, she looked around and discovered that the house was very different from her home in New Jersey. The whole downstairs seemed to be one big room; the kitchen occupied one part and then there was a living room.

Joni remembered Alex had told Mikey that Indians loved fried turtle legs served with pickled spiderwebs. But Mikey was too tired to ask what he was eating, and he just chomped up anything that was put in front of him. There was still no sign of Sarah, and no one even mentioned her name.

Chief Birdsong didn't say much. He just sat at one end of the table and drank his coffee. Dr. McCord was busy asking questions about the clinic. Cartons with extra medical supplies had already been delivered and were stacked in a corner of the Birdsong living room.

Mrs. McCord was asking about the library. She'd have to catalog the books, organize them on shelves, and help train native women to run it.

Joni sighed. She was proud of her parents but sometimes, like now, it was hard to live with them. They were always doing things to help people. The McCords had met in the Peace Corps in South America, where they had volunteered to help dig wells and teach people to read and write. This was before Steven McCord had become a doctor.

That was one of the arguments they had used to convince Joni about the trip. "We live a good life, Joni, and we owe it to society to help others and give things back," Dr. McCord had said.

Joni chewed more slowly. Her eyes were getting heavy. Her body still felt as if it were swaying, like she was still riding in the car. She wondered what her friend Amanda was doing right now.

Sleeping, probably, in her pretty pink and white bedroom. She didn't want to feel like a spoiled brat, but she missed her friends already. Maybe the people on the reservation needed her father to help with their medical problems, and maybe her mother could help with the library, but what was *she* supposed to do for a month?

She was supposed to be friends with a girl who didn't even bother to show up to say hello.

At that very moment, Sarah Birdsong was outside the house with her friends Canada Shenandoah and Oren Lodge. "I'd better go in," Sarah said. "Maw Maw will be angry enough."

Oren tapped the back of the station wagon. "This car was packed with things. It looks like those palefaces are moving in permanently."

"No way," Sarah said. "It's just for one month."

"I wish you could stay with me, Sarah. It's not fair for you to have to share your room," said Canada.

"No. My father wouldn't allow it. I have to be at home."

"Are you going to have to drag that girl around with you to all our summer places?" Oren asked.

"I guess so. You know Indian hospitality. Our house is now their house. Maw Maw will be very angry if I'm not polite."

Oren laughed. "Sure, we have to be polite to

them. But in school or the outside world they call us names and make fun of us."

Canada nodded her head in the dark. "Oren's right. I'll bet she wouldn't be so polite if you were going to *her* house. Remember her stupid letters? This is our land and our rules. She doesn't belong here."

Sarah didn't like the way the conversation was going. "Hey, don't start anything. It's only for one month. I can stand anything for one month."

"Never mind," said Oren. "This girl Joni McCord thinks she knows everything about Indians from cowboy pictures. Well, we've seen those stupid cowboy movies, too. Maybe we should just give her some good memories to take back home when she leaves."

Before Sarah could answer she heard Chief Birdsong. "Is that you, Sarah?"

"Yes, Pa."

"Oren, Canada, go straight home. Your families will be worried. In here now, Sarah. Our guests arrived about forty minutes ago."

Chief Birdsong rested his hand lightly on Sarah's shoulder. Sarah felt her stomach jump. There were so many of them sitting around her kitchen table. A whole family: a mother, father, son, and, yes, that girl who looked about Sarah's size with hair just a little bit lighter. That girl must be Joni McCord.

Seven

The two girls stared at each other. Then they quickly looked to see what each one was wearing. They both had on jeans and T-shirts. Sarah had a wool cardigan sweater wrapped around her waist. Joni wouldn't have to worry about air-conditioning up here. The days were hot and long and lazy, but when the sun went down there was a delightful coolness in the air.

"I saved a sandwich for you, Sarah."

"Thank you, Maw Maw."

When Joni got to know Maw Maw better she would learn to hear the coolness in her voice. The coolness she was now giving to Sarah. Mikey had finished eating and was walking around the living area. "Where's the TV set? Can I watch a program before I go to bed?"

"I'm sorry, son," said Chief Birdsong.

40

"Just one, please?" asked Mikey. "I was real good in the car, Chief. You can ask Mom and Dad. Just one program?"

"I'm sure you were very good, Mikey," answered Chief Birdsong. "You can't watch because we don't have a TV in this house."

Joni glanced over at Sarah, who was chewing her sandwich very slowly and staring at a spot over the window. Up until then Joni hadn't really believed there was no TV, even though Sarah had said so in one of her letters.

"No TV!" Even Mrs. McCord looked surprised, as if she finally realized what no TV would mean to the family. She was probably thinking of Sunday mornings when she and Dr. McCord liked to sleep late, and Mikey was kept quiet by watching early morning cartoons.

Chief Birdsong continued. "We don't like a lot of things from the outside world. We try to keep the traditional ways, the way of the Indian. You will find lots of houses on the reservation that do have TV. Maybe if you make friends you can watch a program somewhere else."

Sarah laughed to herself. Fat chance of that. Both Oren and Canada had TV sets at home, and they would never let any of the McCords in to watch. That's what was so funny. Maw Maw's house, the one house on the reservation that would welcome white people and let them stay, didn't have a TV set to watch. Of course, Sarah

41

had a Walkman. Her mother had sent it to her from the outside. Her pa knew about it, but she tried not to wear it in front of him.

"We have storytellers here, Mikey. And maybe we can tell you some tales so you won't miss your television stories." Maw Maw spoke in that soft voice.

Mikey didn't look too convinced, and — to tell the truth — neither did Joni.

It was time to get everyone ready for bed. Chief Birdsong stood up. "I will probably see you all in the morning. Have a good night." Sarah waited for her pa to come over and give her a good-night hug, but he walked quickly to the front door.

Maw Maw was explaining to Mikey about the trailer next door. It sounded really neat to him. "Oh, can I sleep there? I want to sleep in a trailer! Can I?"

Mrs. McCord finally got him to quiet down. There was a tiny hallway with a bedroom off to the side. Maw Maw opened it and Joni peeked in. There was a large double bed and a dresser. A small pallet was made up on the corner of the floor. That was where Mikey was to sleep.

He was all excited. "Great! I get to sleep with Mom and Dad. Ha ha," he said to Joni. "I get to sleep with Mom and Dad."

Joni didn't think her mother looked all too happy about that arrangement. But Mrs. McCord smiled and put on a bright face. "That's going to be fun,

42

Mikey." Well, thought Joni, her mother and father had been in the Peace Corps in South America, and they had to sleep in much rougher circumstances than just sharing a room with their son.

Sarah had moved down the hall and was standing by a ladder. "Here's where you're going to sleep." It was the first time she had spoken directly to Joni. Her voice was extra tight. She was embarrassed that the house was so small. She knew the McCords probably didn't sleep with Mikey in their room at home. Too bad they couldn't have stayed at Canada's house. Her father owned a big gas station on the highway and was rich. They had a big brick house with all kinds of rooms and fancy furniture. OK. Maw Maw's house was small, but it was big enough for her own family. She was also upset because she didn't want to see anyone sleeping in the bedroom that had belonged to her mother and Pa.

"Take what you need for the night. You can bring the rest of your things up in the morning." Sarah quickly climbed the ladder. It was made of wood, smooth and sanded so there were no rough spots, and it stood firmly on the ground.

"Lucky I'm not afraid of heights." Joni was trying to make a joke, but Sarah didn't answer.

Joni found herself in a large loft that was nestled under the attic eaves. There were two beds side by side. The head of each bed leaned directly against a large window. There were posters on the walls like she had in her own bedroom in New Jersey. But they weren't of rock stars or TV people. There was a picture of a handsome young Indian with a stethoscope around his neck. It had large print that read, WE NEED SOME MODERN MEDICINE MEN.

Even though you had to stoop at the sides of the loft where the roof sloped, you could stand upright in the middle. There was a tiny dressing table tucked in the corner with a comb and brush made with silver handles that had tiny turquoise stones. There were also a couple of lotion bottles, perfume, and a tiny wooden sign that looked as if it had been hand carved. *Property of SARAH BIRDSONG*.

Part of the side wall had been closed off to make a closet. Sarah pointed to it. "There are some extra hangers. You can use them to hang up your clothes."

"Most of my things are downstairs, remember?"

"That's all right. You'll get them tomorrow."

Joni was just holding her small traveling bag. It had her pajamas, soap, and toothpaste. She didn't know what to do next. Was she just supposed to get undressed in front of this stranger? She had never even changed in front of Mandy when they had sleepovers. And they were very best friends.

Sarah pointed to the opposite corner. There was a large wooden screen that Joni hadn't noticed before. "You can change behind there if you want. There's a sink for washing up. But you have to go downstairs to the bathroom."

Joni breathed a sigh a relief. "Oh, that's really neat. You have your own sink right in your room."

Sarah seemed to relax for the tiniest minute. "My pa put it in last year. He's a carpenter. He works for a builder and he does all the fancy cabinets in new houses."

"On the reservation?" asked Joni.

Sarah's face got tight. "No. Not on the reservation. Most of the people here can't afford the houses. They're too expensive. They're for people who live in the suburbs outside the city. Pa has to wake up real early in the morning to get there."

Mikey called up from the bottom of the ladder. "I want to go up and sleep with Joni. I want to climb up the ladder."

Joni gave Sarah a half smile. "He can be a real brat sometimes. It's because he's the baby and everyone spoils him."

"That's OK," Sarah said. "I think he's kind of cute. Sometimes I wish I had a brother or . . ." She caught herself in midsentence. "I'll brush my teeth first if you're going to change."

Joni put on her pajamas as quickly as possible. She couldn't decide whether to go down to the bathroom or not. What if she had to go in the middle of the night? She looked down the ladder. There was a night-light at the foot so she'd be able

45

to see. She didn't know what bed to take, so she hopped from one foot to the other waiting for Sarah to come out.

Sarah was dressed in a long T-shirt and cotton pants. "You can have that one." She pointed to the bed on the left side. Joni climbed in and pulled the quilt up over her. She stared out the window. The moon was hidden again and very few stars were out.

"Is there anything you want before I turn the light out?" asked Sarah.

"No. No, thanks. I'm fine. I've got everything," Joni replied.

Sarah reached from her side of the bed and switched off the light. It was pitch-black. Joni tried to get comfortable on her pillow. She turned it over and over. She could hear Sarah doing the same thing. It was strange sleeping this near to someone. The beds were so close the girls could have held hands across the space.

Joni could hear a faint murmur of voices from downstairs. That made her feel better. Her mother and father were trying to quiet Mikey. For a minute she wished she were the one sleeping in the room with them. She wouldn't feel so strange.

Sarah was also restless listening to Joni tossing and turning. How was she ever going to stay with this stranger for a month? She'd never get to sleep. In two days she'd have circles under her eyes like the raccoons Pa and some of the other hunters caught in the winter.

Joni couldn't get rid of her anxious feeling. When this happened at home, she'd just reach for Raggedy Ann in the dark and hug her until she felt better. Raggedy Ann! The last time she remembered seeing her had been in the car when they had first arrived at the reservation. Maybe the doll was in the living room, piled up with all the suitcases.

She tried to forget about it. But she couldn't. She'd go downstairs and search the living room. Joni tried to get out of bed quietly, searching for the pinpoint of light at the bottom of the ladder.

"I forgot something," she whispered. "I've got to go downstairs."

Sarah didn't answer, just breathed heavily, pretending to be asleep. She thought Joni was probably going down to complain about the room or her bed.

Joni made her way downstairs and into the living room. The boxes and cartons were piled all over the place, but she didn't see the plastic shopping bag or the Raggedy Ann. What if the doll had fallen out of the car? She was afraid to go outside and look. It was so dark.

Joni was deciding whether to ask her father to help her look for Raggedy Ann when she heard a soft voice. "Are you looking for this?" It was Maw

Maw. Her hair hung down her back in one long, black pigtail, and she was wearing a brightly colored robe. She was holding Raggedy Ann.

Joni gasped. "Oh, thanks. How did you know?"

Maw Maw just smiled. "It makes it easier to have something familiar when you're in a strange place."

Joni wanted to ask some more questions but Maw Maw just put her fingers to her lips, as if to say shush, and disappeared into her room, which was at the other side of the kitchen.

Joni climbed back up the ladder and into her bed. She pulled the quilt up under her chin. It was soft and fluffy and smelled of fresh pinecones. There was so much to think about. But she was tired and she missed her New Jersey room. A tree branch knocked against the windowpane and made her jump. Remember, Mom and Daddy are right downstairs, she thought. Joni rubbed her face against Raggedy Ann and hugged her as tightly as she could, as more tree branches brushed against the window.

Sarah never stirred. She was used to the rustling tree branches. This was her home, and they sang her to sleep every night.

Eight

"Hey, Joni. Wake up, it's already morning." Mikey had climbed the ladder and stood at the foot of his sister's bed, pulling at the covers.

"You're sleeping with Raggedy Ann. I see you. I stopped sleeping with my Zeebie a long time ago. And you're still sleeping with your doll."

Mikey's voice and the sun streaming in the window woke Joni. For a moment she couldn't remember where she was. She heard the trees against the window. The reservation — Sarah Birdsong! She quickly stuck Raggedy Ann under the covers. What if Sarah had seen her curled up like a baby with a doll in her arms? But Sarah's bed was empty, and the pillows were fluffed and the quilt was folded neatly.

Joni sat up and wrapped her quilt around her body. She and Mikey heard a creaking noise. It

49

was Sarah climbing back up the ladder.

"How!" Mikey held his hand palm up. "How, Sarah Birdsong. I'm Mikey. That Joni." He pointed to his sister, who was trying to crawl back under the covers and hide. Joni was red with mortification and could have strangled Mikey. That's if Sarah didn't get so insulted she did it first.

"You're on an Indian reservation, not in a Tarzan movie in Africa, little boy," said Sarah. Her father was right. These people spent all their time at the movies or in front of TV sets. They didn't bother to learn how Native Americans really lived. Even the littlest kids picked up stupid ideas.

Joni felt she had to come to Mikey's rescue. "You're right, he's only a little boy. He didn't realize he was insulting."

Sarah was busy opening and closing dresser drawers. "I'm making room for your clothes. Your father wants to put things away."

"Oh, I'll get out of bed." Joni stood up and wrapped the quilt around her waist. "Your room is really nice. It's kind of . . . cozy, I guess."

"You don't have to say things you don't mean. I'm sure you have a giant room in New Jersey. But I like it. It's all mine. My great grandmother made the quilt you've got wrapped around you. It's an heirloom. Some museum people even wanted to put it on display, but my father said no. The government's taken enough stuff away from us already."

Joni quickly unwound the quilt and tried to fold it up as neatly as Sarah's. Mikey followed Sarah around the room as she straightened it and put things away.

"How come your father doesn't live in the same house with you?" he asked.

"He lives right next door in the trailer. That's because he does a lot of work for the Iroquois Nation at home and can spread out his papers. But he comes over here to eat and wash up. There's no running water in the trailer."

"No water? You mean, you turn on a sink and no water comes out? That would be really neat. My mom couldn't make me brush my teeth or wash my hands all day long."

For the first time Sarah had to smile. "No such luck. There's a water pump in the backyard, and you'd have to wash with the outside pump."

"Even in the winter? It must be freezing then!"

Sarah nodded her head, yes. "Sometimes you have to break off icicles before you can use the water."

Mikey's eyes were wide as they could be.

Sarah continued. "We suck on the icicles — they make good ice pops."

"Wow." Mikey looked out the window. "Are there any icicles there today? I want to see."

"No." Sarah laughed. "It's summertime, silly. Too warm for icicles."

"I'm going to ask Daddy if we can stay until winter so I can suck on icicles."

Sarah and Joni looked at each other. Each in her own way was thinking, No — we can't be together until winter — one month is more than enough.

"You have to be very careful of the icicles. They're very sharp. Sharper than knives." Sarah bent over Mikey. Her blue-black hair fell across her shoulders. Her voice was almost a whisper. "Some people use them as knives. SWISSSHHH!" She poked him in the ribs with one finger and he jumped. "A warrior can stick you with an icicle and, while you're lying there bleeding, it melts and no one can figure out what stuck you."

Joni walked over and put her arms around Mikey, who was staring wide-eyed at Sarah. "I don't think it's a good idea to scare a little kid," Joni said. "He won't realize you're kidding."

Sarah stood at the top of the ladder, ready to climb down. She swished her hair back over her shoulders. "Who said I was kidding?"

Joni watched Sarah head downstairs, wondering if the Indian girl was threatening her. That's silly, she thought, and shook herself a few times. Mikey sat on the floor at the foot of the bed, playing with Raggedy Ann. He had her long, narrow rag legs twisted together. Joni went behind the screen and got dressed. She had to put on the same clothes as the day before because her suitcases weren't upstairs yet.

"Don't wreck Raggedy Ann," she yelled from behind the screen.

"I'm just playing," was Mikey's answer.

"Let's go down and have breakfast. I'm starving." Before they started down the ladder Joni took Raggedy Ann away from Mikey. She straightened her bed and was just setting the doll on the pillow when she heard the tree branches against the window. It was the same branch that had kept her awake the night before. A giant old elm with thick branches covered with leaves that circled the roof of the house.

"Mikey!" Joni yelled. She had spotted a face that seemed to float through the tree branches. Her stomach dropped and she grabbed Raggedy Ann from her resting place.

"What's the matter?" Mikey asked. He was on the floor playing with some hand-carved pick-up sticks.

"Go get Daddy. Hurry!" The face glared at her; the eyes seemed to glow a horrible green color. It disappeared for a minute, only to appear closer to the window. The mouth was a bright red slash, and there were matching slashes across the cheeks and forehead.

"Get Daddy!" Joni's voice was a scream.

53

The face had disappeared again — no, there it was at the top of the branch — there were three feathers sticking up from a headdress, and she could see slashes of white paint mixed with red across the cheeks. War paint! Joni jumped back from the window as the face got closer.

"What's going on up here?"

"Daddy!" Joni threw herself in her dad's arms. "The window — it's an Indian with war paint and feathers and this terrible look in his eyes."

"What are you talking about?" Chief Birdsong and Sarah climbed into the room.

Dr. McCord pointed to the window. His voice sounded embarrassed. "Joni thought she saw something out the window."

" 'Thought'!" Joni picked her head up from Dr. McCord's chest, where she had it buried. "I saw it! I saw it! I did. Ask . . ." She looked around the room. Sarah hadn't been there. "Ask Mikey. He was here with me."

"But Joni," said Mikey. "You made me go downstairs for Daddy. Where's that Indian? I'll get him for you."

Chief Birdsong had the window wide open and leaned all the way out, bending the tree branches every which way. "You saw an Indian here, this morning? Can you point out where?"

Holding onto her father's hand, Joni walked back to the window. The sun was shining brightly and a soft breeze gently moved the tree leaves. She looked up at the highest branch and down to the ground. There was no floating Indian face with green eyes and war paint. There was nothing at all.

Sarah crawled through the window onto the roof. She climbed onto one of the limbs and worked her way down to the ground. "Nothing here, Pa," she called up to Chief Birdsong.

"Come back up, Sarah," her pa answered, then turned to Joni. "Sometimes when you are very tired and in a new place, you imagine things that you are afraid of. There's nothing there and our house is safe." He nodded his head at Dr. McCord and made his way back downstairs.

"Daddy, I *did* see the face. It was an Indian in war paint, staring at me."

Sarah came back through the window and looked at Joni. Her voice was very flat. "There's nothing outside and I didn't see any footprints around the tree. So whatever you saw must fly because it sure doesn't walk." Sarah followed Chief Birdsong down the ladder.

Dr. McCord took Raggedy Ann out of Joni's hand and put her back on the pillow. "Well, Raggedy Ann looks comfortable. Just like at home."

Joni was embarrassed. Her dad had turned into Dr. McCord the pediatrician. He was using his doctor's voice, the one he used to speak to children

in his office. "I'm sure you thought you saw something, Joni. But it was a long trip yesterday and
you were very tired."

"I did see it, Daddy, I did. I'm not crazy, you
know."

"No one said you were. Maybe you did see
something. The sun could have reflected off the
window or the roof in a crazy way."

"To turn into an Indian warrior in war paint."

"Well, then, maybe it was an animal — a cat —
you said you thought the eyes were green."

"A cat in feathers?" It was no use. Joni felt like
screaming. No one was going to believe her. She
wished she could call Amanda back in New Jersey. It was no use talking to Sarah. She was the
one who had originally talked about people
disappearing.

"OK, Daddy, I don't want to talk about it anymore. Maybe you're right."

Dr. McCord gave Joni a hug. "Good girl. But
just remember, I'm here, and you call me or your
mother anytime you're worried about something.
Even Indian faces appearing in the treetops."

Nine

"Wow! Look at all this stuff!" Mikey was in a small alcove off the living room. Joni didn't remember seeing it the night before. There were pictures of Indian families on the walls. There were masks and a collection of tomahawks and knives. An old glass cabinet held all kinds of beads and fancy jewelry. Necklaces of colored Indian corn hung on nails. It looked like a museum — even though it was small. Just like the Indian section of the big museum in New York City.

Sarah and Maw Maw followed Mikey. "I must ask you to be very careful in here. These things" — Maw Maw waved her hands around the room — "belonged to my ancestors and they're very precious to me."

Sarah proudly opened a large hand-carved chest. Pine and other forest smells filled the air.

57

The chest was packed with beautiful quilts. "These were made by our ancestors. Like the one you slept under last night," she said.

Mikey had his hands on some beaded belts that were hanging in the corner. "What's this?" Little five-year-old hands can be very rough, even when they don't mean to be. Sarah Birdsong quickly grabbed Mikey's hands. "Those are wampum beads, Mikey. You have to be very, very careful with them."

Maw Maw nodded. "Before you go back to New Jersey I'll explain everything that's in the room to you, but right now, it's time for breakfast."

Sarah reached for some carved figures that were on one of the high shelves. She looked at Maw Maw, who nodded yes. "Here, Mikey." She handed him a small bird that was hand carved out of bone and polished until it shone. "This is our family crest. It's a little bird and his mouth is open so he's singing. You'll always remember our name: Birdsong."

"Wow, that's really neat. I'm going to show Daddy." He stopped and looked at Sarah. "Can I really keep it for my very own?" Sarah smiled back yes.

Joni wondered as she followed Sarah into breakfast. Sarah had gotten awful nice since Joni had seen the face at the window. It was almost as if she were trying to make up, or maybe throw Joni off guard. After all, Sarah hadn't been in the room at the time. Could she have been the face? Maybe, but then how would she have washed all that paint off so quickly before she returned to the room?

Joni wanted some breakfast. She'd have a bad headache if she had to think this hard all the time she was up here.

Everyone had breakfast together, except for Chief Birdsong, who had tribal business to attend to. Sarah slapped some jelly on a piece of bread, stood up, kissed Maw Maw, and started for the door.

"Sarah!" Maw Maw's voice was quiet but firm. "Where are you running off to? Remember, we have guests in our house." Then Maw Maw spoke to Sarah in the language of the Senecas.

"Yes, Maw Maw." Sarah sighed and turned to Joni. "After you put your things away, I'll show you around, if you want me to."

"Oh, that would be so nice," said Mrs. McCord. "Wouldn't it, Joni?"

Everyone waited for Joni's answer. Grown-ups! They're so sure they know everything. Just because two girls are the same age and in the same school grade and are thrown together doesn't mean they're going to be friends.

Now Joni matched Sarah's sigh. "Sure. That'll be great." Mrs. McCord smiled and looked over at Dr. McCord, as if to say, See? Everything is going to be fine. But Maw Maw sat quietly, a tiny frown line forming on her forehead as she studied the two girls carefully.

It took a while for the McCord family to get organized. They had brought too many things. There weren't enough closets for all the clothes, and Sarah had to get some clean cardboard boxes for Joni to stack her shirts and underwear in.

Mrs. McCord called Joni into the bedroom to ask for some help. She closed the door and asked Joni to sit down on the bed. She found her hairbrush and began brushing Joni's hair. She always did this when she wanted to have a serious discussion. Mrs. McCord always had to be touching her children to make sure they understood that what she was about to say was for their own good. "I know it was hard for you to leave Amanda and New Jersey. But if you keep an open mind, this month can be an event that you will treasure for the rest of your life."

Joni just nodded and closed her eyes. She loved for her mother to brush her hair. It felt so good she would usually agree to anything.

"Do you realize that the Birdsong family is very prominent?" her mother asked Joni. "The Iroquois are actually six separate nations. But they have the same laws and culture. It's as if six different families were living under one roof. As if all our cousins, the ones in Brooklyn and California, all followed the same rules." Mrs. McCord had done

60

a lot of studying before she came to the reservation, and she was determined to learn more and have Joni do so also.

"Try to remember to say Native American instead of Indian, Joni. The reservation is part of the Iroquois Nation, and they consider it their own country, separate from the United States. The Iroquois live on fourteen reservations in the United States and Canada. They've had so much land taken away from them throughout history that they don't trust the government too much. They see the world divided in two. The Native world and the non-Native."

The hair brushing went on as Mrs. McCord kept talking. But for once it wasn't soothing Joni the way it usually did. Why did she have to worry or care about Natives and non-Natives? She was only going to be here for a month. What could she do about it?

There was a knock on the door. "It's me, Mrs. McCord," said Sarah. "Maw Maw has some more clean boxes for you."

"Come in," Mrs. McCord called out. Before Joni had a chance to move, Sarah walked into the room. She took in the whole scene. Joni leaning against her mother, having her shiny brown hair brushed out. Sarah's face stiffened, and she felt a pang in her chest right near the spot where her heart beat. She remembered a scene not too long ago in this very room on that bed. Another girl sat, her hair just a little bit darker than Joni McCord's. That girl had also leaned against a mother who had a soft voice and softer hands, who smelled like a spring garden, and gently brushed and braided a little girl's hair into two dark plaits.

"Here are your boxes." Sarah slammed them in the corner and ran out of the room.

Joni sat up quickly. "She's always doing that. One minute she's nice, and then she acts all mean and impatient."

Mrs. McCord put her brush away. Joni stood up and reached for the fresh boxes. "I mean, we weren't doing anything. I was just sitting here getting my hair brushed. Why should that get her all upset?"

Ten

It took most of the morning for the McCords to get settled. Joni had mixed feelings. She wanted to get outside and see what the reservation was like, yet she was afraid of that face she had seen outside her window. It had been there, no matter what Dr. McCord and Chief Birdsong said. Mikey kept forgetting there was no TV and every once in a while he'd ask to see a program. Joni wondered how long a modern person could go without TV. Dr. McCord said there were studies in his medical journals of people who had shut the TV off for years without any bad effects.

Joni had another shock when she asked if she could make a phone call. Whenever she closed her eyes she could see that face in the window. She wanted to talk it over with her friend Amanda. She promised to pay for the long distance call herself. Out of her own allowance. Maw Maw said that the telephone was in the house just for emergencies and because Dr. McCord might be called. She hoped that Joni would understand that no one else was to use it. Joni felt as if she had been zapped again, with another privilege that she had been used to taken away.

Joni wondered if there was a telephone in the trailer. She didn't suppose so. If the chief didn't have running water, he probably wouldn't have a telephone.

Some of Sarah's friends came by before lunch. She didn't invite them in or introduce them to Joni. As a matter of fact, she went outside to talk. Joni watched them laughing and joking around a big pine tree in the front yard. She felt jealous when she saw Sarah looking relaxed and smiling. There were two boys and two girls. At one point they burst into laughter and put their arms around each other. They laughed so hard they fell to the ground.

"Shh." Sarah pointed to the house and put her fingers to her lips to keep them quiet. Joni tried to move back from the window before the group of kids saw her. One boy looked a little familiar. She tried to picture him in war paint and feathers.

When Sarah came back in the house she asked Joni if she wanted to take a walk. Joni really wasn't sure. But the sun was shining and without a TV or telephone she didn't want to stay cooped up. Dr. and Mrs. McCord were going to go food shopping. That was part of the rental arrangement. They would be paying all the food bills. Maw Maw was going to go with them, since the nearest big supermarket was forty miles away.

Sarah kissed Maw Maw good-bye and the girls started off. Joni turned back once to wave at Mrs. McCord, who was on the front porch steps. The two girls looked pretty similar. They both wore jeans and T-shirts and sneakers. Almost like a uniform. The same way Joni would dress to go for a walk in New Jersey with her friends. Only in New Jersey they wouldn't be walking. One of the moms would drive them to the mall. They'd walk around the stores, looking in the windows and buying snacks.

Sarah wore her hair loose. She had a red and white checked bandanna around her neck. Around the edges there was delicate red and white beading, and she wore matching long beaded earrings.

"That's really pretty." Joni broke the silence by pointing to the kerchief.

"Thanks." Sarah turned off the main road onto an unplowed field. Joni tried to study the area. There was the main unpaved road and some houses. There were houses like Sarah's and then there were trailers. Most of the driveways weren't paved, but there were cars all over the place. Even if a house didn't have a TV antenna it seemed to have a couple of cars in the front yard. Some of the cars didn't even look as if they worked. They were rusting and the wheels were off.

One house they passed looked like a junkyard. Not only did it have a collection of cars in the front but it also had broken down washers and dryers.

Joni wanted to ask why all these things were left lying around, but she didn't want Sarah to get mad.

Sarah was used to her surroundings so she didn't even notice. Joni went back to the kerchief. "Is that beading special? I mean, like . . ." She tried to remember what her mother had said. "I mean, is that a special Native American design?"

Sarah stopped, bent over, and broke off a long, dried twig that she put in her mouth. After sucking a few minutes she said, "Where were you born?"

Joni's stomach dropped. She must have made another mistake. It seemed she was as bad as Mikey, asking stupid questions. "I was born in New Jersey, why?"

"And where's New Jersey?"

"In America, of course!"

"Good!" Sarah clapped her hands together as if she were applauding a correct answer. "So you're a Native American. I was born on Woodland Reservation in New York State, U.S.A., so I'm a Native American, too. But I'm also part of the Iroquois Nation. So you can call me an Indian."

Joni was totally confused and getting a little annoyed. "You don't have to take my head off. My mom thought your people didn't like to be called Indians."

"If you want to know what I like or don't like, why don't you ask me?"

"OK, I will."

Sarah climbed over a rough wooden fence that separated waving cornfields. She jogged through the rows. This was just like follow the leader, thought Joni, except Sarah had clammed up again.

The girls walked a little farther in silence. Joni took a breath. "No matter what, I still like that beading. And I don't care if it's Native-American-Tribal-Iroqouis-Pennsylvania-New York-New Jersey-United States of America-Planet Earth-or Global Galaxy beading!" She let her breath out and Sarah started to laugh.

"I'll bet you can't say that again."

"I could say it if I could remember it."

Both the girls laughed and Sarah pointed to a slope that led to a field below them. Sarah had taken a chance on taking Joni there. It was one of her favorite places. What if Joni laughed or was bored? There were thousands and thousands of wildflowers, all colors and shapes and sizes. Corn-flower-blue jump-ups tumbled next to blackeyed daisies, and tiny purple stars formed a magic carpet on some green moss that sprouted leaf-shaped flowers. It was better than any mall.

"Oh, it's gorgeous," Joni cried.

"We come here and make wildflower bouquets, dry them, and sell them in the market in Buffalo," said Sarah.

It had gotten warmer. The sun was directly overhead and there was a soft haze over the flowers. Butterflies darted back and forth, and there was the low hum of bees in the air. A sweet smell hung over everything.

Sarah pointed to some bushy, vine-like trees at the edge of the field. "Honeysuckle," she said. "If you pick some and dry them out and put them in jars with other herbs and flowers, they make potpourri just like they sell in fancy department stores."

"Oh, let's do it. I'd like to bring some home for my friends."

For the next few minutes the girls picked flowers side by side.

Sarah pointed to her neck. "This beading you like? My mother made it. She's really good with her hands."

"That's right, we didn't meet your mother yet."

Sarah went back to the flowers. She pushed Joni's hands away from some fuchsia stalks that had hidden thorns on the stems. "My mother doesn't live with us right now. She's in Washington, D.C. Lots of Indian families have people that live off the reservation. They work and send back money. She's a secretary and goes to college. She wants to be a social worker."

"Oh, that's neat. I guess it's hard, though; you must miss her."

"Yes." Sarah moved slightly away from Joni. That should have been Joni's warning not to ask any more questions. But she was relaxed, the air smelled sweet, and the flowers in her hands were beautiful. "So does your mom come home on vacations?"

"No. Not for a while." Sarah had her head down and her voice was muffled. Once again Joni should have been warned to keep her mouth shut.

"That's terrible. Does that mean your mom and dad are going to get a divorce? Half the kids in my class have parents that are divorced."

"No! They're not getting a divorce. I knew you wouldn't understand. My pa and his family are traditional. They want to stay on the reservation and hand down our culture. And, well, my mother — she doesn't want to live here. She wants to be out in the world."

"Wow. That's pretty heavy stuff. Who would you rather live with, your mom or your dad?"

Sarah turned and pelted Joni with the flowers

in her hand. "Boy, for a paleface, you sure have a big mouth."

"I do not. Look." Joni pursed her lips together and made them real small and tight.

"Well, maybe your mouth is small but you sure have a big tongue."

"Do not." Joni stuck it out as far as it could go.

"Do so." Sarah had emptied all the flowers in her arms, and now she grabbed some dandelion fluff and blew the white stuff in Joni's face. "Big tongue and bird legs."

"Bird legs?" Joni looked down at her legs, but they were covered in jeans.

"I saw those skinny bird legs last night when you got out of bed."

Now it was Joni's chance to pelt Sarah with the flowers in her arms.

Sarah ducked, laughing. "I think I'll give you an Indian name — Joni Bird Legs."

"What kind of name is that?"

"A good Iroquois name for a nosy paleface. Or would you rather be called Joni With Tongue That Wags?"

"I don't like either name. But if I have bird legs, you'd better run for it."

Joni started to chase Sarah, who zigzagged across the field of flowers. They ran up and down and sideways and across, until they both tumbled down out of breath and sweating at the end of the field. Both girls rolled over and over on the velvety moss.

It was fun to lie still, catch their breath, and look up at the sky. Something was tickling Joni's hand.

"Don't brush it off. Don't move," said Sarah in a stern voice.

Joni looked down. There was a large bug walking on her right hand.

"Yuck!"

"No! Let it alone. It's a walking stick. Watch it. If you let it walk up one arm and down the other you'll live a long time."

Joni held her breath as the insect slowly made its way up her right arm, across her chest, and started down the left arm.

"This is real crucial now," whispered Sarah. "If he falls off before he reaches your other hand, your life will be short."

Joni thought she was kidding, but just in case, she held her breath as the insect wobbled a little on her elbow before making its way down across her left hand and onto her thumb, and then back into the grass of the field.

"Whew!" Joni blew air out of her cheeks and stood up. "I made it through that. I'd better not take a chance on another one."

"See, Joni Bird Legs? It's lucky you came up to Woodland. We've got lots of things to teach you."

Sarah blew another dandelion fluff at Joni and took off across the field.

Sarah spread her arms out like a huge bird and zigzagged back and forth. Joni had no trouble following behind. She spread her arms out, too. After all, she was Joni Bird Legs and, besides, the walking stick had just told her she was going to live a very long life!

Eleven

Joni chattered happily on the way back to the Birdsong house.

"Would you like a cold soda?" asked Sarah.

"Sure. It's really hot out. But where?" She looked around the open fields. There was no main street that she could see where there would be stores or even a movie theater.

Sarah pointed to a small log house that was practically hidden by large trees. They walked up the dirt driveway, where a lot of cars and pickup trucks were parked. Joni was getting used to seeing new cars and old junks in driveways and front yards. A small tarpaper shack was attached to the side of the house. There were signs advertising cigarettes, candy, and soft drinks. Canada Shenandoah and Oren Lodge, along with two other of Sarah's friends, Florrie Greeneyes and

Nathan Mohawk, were sitting around drinking Cokes.

Sarah ran toward her friends. "Is this where you were all day?"

"Where have you been?" asked Canada. "We went past your house before but no one was home."

There was nothing for Joni to do but follow Sarah, who didn't bother to introduce anyone. "I told you I had to show" — Sarah pointed at Joni — "around this afternoon." The sweet, laughing Sarah from the wildflower field disappeared as she talked to her friends. She acted as if Joni were a complete stranger who had wandered onto the reservation.

Joni backed away from Sarah and her friends. She rubbed her sneaker in the dirt and kept her head down, as if she were studying rock formations. She could feel the eyes of the Indian children as they studied her from head to toe. It was like being in a zoo where invisible bars kept her from getting away. She couldn't go, even though she wanted to, because she didn't know her way back to the Birdsong house.

"So, is this your visitor, Sarah?" asked Oren.

Joni wished she had her Raggedy Ann with her right now. It would feel so good to hold something close for comfort. Instead she made a fist so hard with her right hand that her nails dug into the palm. That way she could concentrate on how she was pinching herself rather than on the kids who were staring her down.

Nathan Mohawk took a step forward. "You're not even supposed to be living on the reservation. It's only for enrolled Indian families. The only reason you're allowed to sleep here is because your father is running the clinic for Dr. Ken."

That was news to Joni. Now she found out that the McCords weren't even supposed to be living on the reservation. Wait until she told her father. But that still didn't explain why everyone was so nasty.

She tried to tough it out. "Is this where we can get a cold drink, Sarah?" Joni reached for the handle of the old screen door.

Oren Lodge stepped in front of her. "No pale-faces allowed in there. Sorry."

Joni took a step backward. She felt as if she'd just had her face slapped. Sarah stood in a tight circle with her friends. They leaned against one another. It was like a flock of birds that were flying south, joined by other birds of the same type. Joni thought of the old saying, "Birds of a feather flock together." It didn't seem as if Joni Bird Legs belonged with Sarah Birdsong.

Finally Sarah broke the staring contest. "Oh, come on. Let's go in and get a drink." Joni breathed a sigh of relief and followed Sarah into the little store. There was a large glass refrigerator filled with cold cans of soda. Small wooden shelves were stocked with candy, chips, and other snacks. Sarah's friends followed the girls into the store.

Sarah opened the refrigerator. "What would you like?"

Before Joni could answer, Canada Shenandoah spoke up. "We're here to make sure that strangers on the reservation don't do any shoplifting."

"That's right," agreed Florrie Greeneyes, who had the most spectacular green eyes trimmed with the blackest of eyelashes. Green eyes! Joni thought that was odd. It reminded her of something, but before she could think it through, Oren piped up. "We have to be very careful of the people we allow on the reservation. There's been a lot of heavy stealing going on!"

Joni felt her cheeks stain red as she realized they were talking about her! Did they think she was a shoplifter? Just because she was different from them, did they think she would steal?

She reached into her pocket hoping that the crumpled dollar Dr. McCord had given her was still there. "Here." She pulled it out and put it on the counter. "I'll just have an orange soda."

Oren picked up the bill and threw it to Nathan. "Did you see a dollar bill?"

Nathan pitched it behind his back to Florrie Greeneyes. "No, I didn't. What about you, Sarah?"

When the dollar bill reached Sarah she grabbed it and put it on the counter near the register with some change of her own. She threw the can of orange soda at Joni. "Come on, we'd better go. Maw Maw will murder me if anything happens to you."

Joni shivered even though they were out in the hot sun. The metal can of soda was cold and sweated droplets of water down the sides.

"I'll see you guys later." Before they could leave, Canada grabbed Sarah and pulled her back to the storefront. Joni put her head down again and followed the dirt driveway back out to the road. Maybe, she thought, if she got to the main road she could find her way back to the Birdsong house. She looked over her shoulder once. Sarah had her arms around her friends and they looked as if they were involved in a football huddle, giving each other signals.

Joni heard running feet come after her. "What did you run away for?" It was Sarah. She had opened her own can of soda and was taking long sips. Joni shook her head. Maybe the heat had fried her brains. She'd better drink some of her own soda.

"What am I running for? Your friends practically accused me of being a thief! How did you think I'd feel?"

Sarah took another drink. "To tell the truth, I really didn't think about it. Now you know how Indian kids feel when we go shopping or to a mall and storekeepers say, 'Hey, don't touch anything, you dirty Indians!' Or they follow and watch us

77

as if we were going to blow up the place!"

"But that's not my fault. Why are you taking it out on me?"

"Because you're here. Why don't you go back to New Jersey, where you belong? Go back to your friend Amanda, and your town swimming pool, and your TV, and your telephone. And take your stupid rag doll with you!"

Twelve

Joni took a deep breath and swallowed. She tried to speak but couldn't even think of any words to say. There was nothing to do but follow Sarah down the dirt road and try to stop the tears gathering in her eyes.

The girls walked the rest of the way in silence. Joni following Sarah back across cornfields, backyards, and over and under fences. Sarah couldn't find any words to say, either. Why had she said those things to Joni? It always happened when she was around her friends. They made her feel as if she were a traitor for even walking with this outsider. She thought how angry Maw Maw would be if she found out. And her pa. As chief he had invited Joni and her family to be guests in his house. And Joni was still a guest, even though they were outdoors.

Sarah stared up at the sky. She remembered walking with her mother to pick strawberries for the summer festival. Her mother had said they were practicing the Indian Way. Indians were supposed to protect Mother Earth and live in her house. The ground was the floor and the sky was the ceiling. Sarah felt herself tightening up. Sure, her mother had talked about the Indian Way, but she had left the reservation and Sarah behind.

When they reached the Birdsong yard, Sarah turned and grabbed Joni's arm. "I suppose you're going to run and tell your father."

Joni pulled her arm away. "Tell him what? I'm not a squealer. I don't care about you and your friends anyway."

Sarah stared at Joni. Maybe she should apologize. She didn't want Maw Maw and Pa to be upset with her. But it was hard to forget what her friends had just said to her. "You'd better not bring that girl with you to any of our secret places."

"Remember," said Nathan. "She's in your house and in your room and she'll take everything away from you. Just like the white man's always taken everything from us."

Sarah's friends didn't have to worry. She knew the history of her people too well. And if she ever did forget, Pa was right there to remind her. Remind her how her ancestors had helped the white people to settle the country. The Birdsongs were descended from Chief Skenendore, an Oneida chief, part of the Iroquois Nation who brought 300 bushels of white Indian corn to George Washington at Valley Forge. Sarah wondered if Joni learned that in her school in New Jersey. If the Indians hadn't shown the colonial army how to cook it, they wouldn't have lasted the winter.

And what reward did the Indians get? They were pushed off their own lands and moved around and around the country until they wound up on reservations. And most of the time reservations were made up of parcels of land that nobody else wanted anyway.

"Well." Mrs. McCord opened the front porch door. "Welcome back. You girls look all flushed from the sun. We're practically settled. Maw Maw helped us shop and we're just about all unpacked."

Dr. McCord had been reading the paper, but he smiled at the girls and his eyes met his wife's. See? his eyes seemed to say. The girls are getting along fine. They just needed a little time to get acquainted.

Maw Maw was setting the table. She was not fooled that easily. Too many bad vibrations had come in the door with the girls. Their afternoon had not gone as smoothly as it looked on the surface.

"Boo!" Mikey jumped out from behind the door.

"Boo yourself," said Sarah over her shoulder as she ran to the back of the house and up the ladder stairs. Joni could hear the floor door to the loft slam. She wanted to change her shirt. It was all sweaty and there were grass stains down the back and some drips of orange soda. But she wasn't going to take the chance of being alone with Sarah again. She'd wait until Sarah came out of the room.

She wandered into the alcove where Maw Maw had all her Indian things. Mikey followed along. "Do you see that tomahawk, Joni?" He leaned over and whispered to his sister, "How many people do you think that tomahawk scalped?"

Joni suddenly remembered the face outside her window that morning and she shivered as she stared at the sharp edge of the tomahawk. Maw Maw had followed them into the room. "I think you should know, Mikey, that Indians did not invent scalping. Nor were they the only ones to practice it. As a matter of fact, French fur traders scalped their victims."

Mikey didn't care about any history lessons. He was just itching to get the tomahawk in his hands.

Sarah reappeared. She had washed and changed her clothes. She had even brushed out her hair and braided it down her back. "I'm going to see if Pa's in the trailer, Maw Maw. He promised that we'd eat together tonight." Sarah had taken off the beaded kerchief. Around her neck was a thin silver chain that held a small turtle with turquoise and coral stones in its back.

Mikey noticed it first. "You've got a turtle around your neck."

Sarah smiled and touched it. "Yes."

Maw Maw touched it, too, and smiled. She leaned over and patted her granddaughter on the head. "Go along with you now. I'll see you later at Longhouse."

"What's a Longhouse?" asked Mikey.

Sarah got uptight again. "It's our religion. We're People of the Longhouse — it's our traditional way."

Joni wouldn't give Sarah the satisfaction of hearing her ask any questions, but she was glad that Mikey did.

"Why do you call your religion 'Longhouse'?"

"Because our ceremonies and our meetings where all our laws are read are held in a long wooden house."

"Like a church?"

"I guess you could say so. We've got a stove in the middle — there used to be an open fire in the olden days. Then there are benches, and the men sit on one side and the women on the other," Sarah said.

"Can I see it?"

"You can see it from the outside. But non-Natives are not allowed in."

Joni forgot she wasn't going to speak to Sarah. "But why not? If you were in New Jersey you could come to a church or a temple."

Sarah jumped back at her. "I knew you wouldn't understand. Ask my grandmother or my father if you want to know anything else." Sarah turned away and stormed out the door, slamming it hard.

Again Joni felt as if she had had her face slapped. Sarah was like one of those purple wild-flowers in the field. Pretty and soft-looking on the outside and then — zap — loaded with thorns on the stem.

Well, she was gone now and Joni could change for dinner. Maw Maw and Chief Birdsong were nice and friendly, but Sarah wasn't. Maybe she could write to Amanda and get invited to stay at her house for the rest of the month. Then her parents and Mikey could stay here, Sarah could have her room back and hang around with her friends, and Joni would be at the town pool. Everyone would be happy!

She left Mikey staring at the tomahawk and climbed the ladder to the bedroom. Sarah was very neat. There were no signs of her dirty clothes. No signs that she had even been in the room.

Joni flopped on her bed. She was almost too tired to change for dinner. She lay on her back. The window behind the two beds was open. There was just a tiny breeze, and the room under the eaves was still hot from the strong sun. Joni reached behind her for Raggedy Ann. She wondered whether Sarah had seen her sleeping with the doll the night before. Well, so what? Lots of people had a favorite animal or toy. Not sixth-graders probably. At least, not tough sixth-grade Indian girls.

That was funny. She couldn't feel Raggedy. She sat up and searched behind the pillow, under the pillow, and all over the bed. No doll. She got off the bed and searched underneath. Raggedy might have slipped off. Again nothing. Her heart was starting to beat a little faster. She was positive she had left her on the bed. What could have happened?

Slow down, she told herself. Raggedy has to be there someplace. Joni searched the room from top to bottom. She looked in the corner of the eaves, and searched through all the drawers in the hope that the doll had accidentally gotten tucked away. She sifted through the clothes hanging on the open hooks. She searched the bookshelves and, as a last resort, leaned out the window. Her face was in the middle of the branches and all she saw were green leaves. No spot of color that even looked like a rag doll.

Joni slowly drew her head back into the room and leaned against her pillow. Slowly the tears she had been holding in all day ran down her cheeks and soaked into the pillowcase. Raggedy Ann had been with her since she was two years old. Through a trip to the hospital to have her tonsils out and the time a nasty baby-sitter had slapped her. She woke up with Raggedy Ann and went to sleep with her, and during the day the doll waited patiently on her bed. Now the doll was gone and so was Sarah Birdsong.

Thirteen

Joni pulled herself together and rolled off the bed. She wasn't a squealer but she needed to talk to someone about Raggedy Ann. She went to the top of the ladder. She could hear voices downstairs. "Mom," she called. No answer. "Daddy?" The voices were coming from the living room. They were probably so involved in conversation that nobody could hear her.

She went to the little sink in the corner and wiped her face. Sarah had told her to leave and take her stupid doll with her. I guess Sarah couldn't wait, Joni thought. *She* decided to take my doll first.

Joni went down the ladder and stood at the corner of the living room. "Daddy? Mom?" Dr. McCord turned. "What's the matter, Joni? Come on in, we're all getting acquainted."

87

The "all" were Maw Maw, Chief Birdsong, and the Indian men they had met the first night. Sarah was nowhere in sight. She had told Maw Maw she was going to be with her father that night, and he was sitting in plain sight in the living room.

"Could I please see you a minute, Daddy?"

Dr. McCord frowned, then excused himself and came into the hall. "What's the matter, Joni?" He tilted her head back. "Why are your eyes so red? Have you been crying?"

Well, at least he was finally noticing something around here besides his plans for the clinic. "My Raggedy Ann . . ." Joni couldn't help it. The tears started all over again. In between sobs she tried to explain to her father what had happened.

"Are you sure you had it with you?"

"Of course, I am. I had it in the back of the car!"

"That's right. But maybe it's still in one of the suitcases?"

"No, Daddy, I slept with it last night. And I had it this morning on my bed. Remember, you even said she looked comfortable."

"Let's take another look. You must have moved her." Joni followed her father back up the ladder and stood with her arms folded while he searched the room all over again. He was sweating when he finished. Then he insisted upon going down-stairs into a corner closet where their suitcases were stored. He went through all of them.

Chief Birdsong walked in at one point. "Is something wrong, Doctor? Can I be of help?"

"No, thanks. Joni thinks she might have misplaced something. I'm just going out to check the car."

Joni was mortified. Chief Birdsong was staring right at her. She didn't want him to know about this. He already thought she was crazy for seeing the face in the window this morning.

Dr. McCord came back into the room. "The car was clean. It wasn't in there. Let's go outside for a minute, Joni." He put his arm around her shoulders and walked her to the corner of the yard. "I don't think we should say anything about this, Joni. After all, you have no proof that Sarah took it."

"Proof! Who else went up to the loft? I don't think Maw Maw would want it." Squealer or no squealer, she was ready to tell him how Sarah and her friends had acted, when he held up his hand.

"I know this is difficult for you. But it's just a doll. I'll get you a brand-new one when you get home. The work your mother and I are going to do is important. And it's important for you to make friends. Just give it time."

Joni felt the tears again. Just a doll! And her father was supposed to be a great pediatrician who understood children! She had heard him tell millions of mothers not to worry if their children liked to sleep with a favorite thing. But he was telling *her* Raggedy Ann was just a doll!

Maw Maw called everyone to the dinner table. Dr. McCord walked Joni inside, his hands firmly on her shoulders. Everyone sat and Maw Maw began serving. No one mentioned that Sarah wasn't there.

"What kind of meat is in this stew?" asked Dr. McCord. "Or have you used special spices? It has a very strong, gamey taste. Delicious."

Chief Birdsong answered quietly. "It's deer meat."

Mrs. McCord put her fork down. She was practically a vegetarian anyway, and she would never wear a fur coat because she was against killing animals.

"Are we eating Bambi?" asked Mikey.

Chief Birdsong had a gentle singsong rhythm to his voice. "Woodland Indians are natural hunters, and we've passed on our skills from father to son. We live close to the land and we hunt and fish. But we don't do it for fun. We don't make trophies and hang them on the wall. The animal has a spirit, so we kill him quickly and as painlessly as we can and use him for food. We believe we were put here to protect the land and guard it."

"Well." Dr. McCord cleared his throat and looked around the table. He motioned for Mikey and Joni to continue eating but Mrs. McCord seemed to have trouble swallowing.

Joni wasn't hungry. She just wanted to get away from the table as soon as it was polite. Just *wait* until Sarah returned. She'd have it out with her.

The side door flew open. It was Sarah. She was out of breath and was holding a brown paper bag. Joni dropped her fork. It looked about the size that would hold a doll. She watched carefully as Sarah put it on a shelf in the living room.

"I'm sorry, Maw Maw, that our plans got all mixed up." Sarah sat next to her father and spooned herself some stew.

"Excuse me." Joni got up from the table and acted as if she were walking toward the bathroom. When she was sure that everyone was busy eating she snatched the brown paper bag and made for the loft ladder. Once upstairs she opened the bag quickly. There was a shirt and what looked like leggings all folded up. She turned the bag inside out. There was no Raggedy Ann. She heard a voice calling out. Sarah had climbed after her and stood on the top rung.

"Would you mind telling me what you're doing with my things?"

Fourteen

The two girls stared at each other. "What am I doing with your things?" Joni screeched. "Where's my Raggedy Ann doll?"

"I don't know what you're talking about."

"My doll that I sleep with."

"That babyish thing with the red hair? How would I know? I'm grown up. I don't sleep with dolls."

"It was up here on the bed and now it's gone."

Sarah flopped down on her own bed. "How am I supposed to know where it is?"

"You're the only one up here, and I don't believe in ghosts or spirits."

"I told you I don't know where your doll is."

"Well, if *you* didn't take it, then who did?"

"Maybe the same Indian that you saw floating

through the trees this morning." Sarah went back downstairs and didn't return until it was time for bed. The girls changed into their pajamas without talking.

Joni had trouble falling asleep. She tossed and turned. She'd reach out for Raggedy Ann, forgetting that the doll wasn't there anymore. She watched the moon through the window and finally her eyes closed. She dreamed of the yarn-haired Raggedy Ann but just as she reached for her, the doll was snatched away by a pair of waving hands that were attached to a floating face wearing Indian war feathers.

Once she thought she heard a quiet voice from Sarah's bed. "I really didn't take your doll, Joni. No matter what you think. I really didn't take it." But they were just words in the dark, and by morning Joni didn't even remember hearing them.

It rained for the next two days, so it was hard to do much exploring of the reservation. Dr. McCord opened the clinic and he was very busy. Joni tried to visit, but when she saw the long line of patients she knew her father wouldn't have time for her. Mrs. McCord was busy at the library and Joni, Sarah, and Mikey spent one afternoon unpacking and dusting books to put on the shelves.

Mikey was getting bored, so Mrs. McCord told

the girls to take him back to the house. They wore ponchos because the rain came down like curtains, and the dirt road turned into a mud stream. Sarah stopped, took off her sneakers, and rolled up her jeans. She splashed in the gully by the side of the road. Of course, Mikey was a copycat and after watching the two of them splash down the block, Joni took her own shoes off. The air was warm and Joni's toes sunk into the rich, dark mud. She wiggled them around and laughed. She hadn't forgotten Raggedy Ann, but it was hard to be mad when the warm rain was washing your face and your toes were digging into Mother Earth.

By the third day of rain everyone was getting a little crazy. Sarah's friends hadn't come around and she couldn't phone them. They were probably meeting at each other's houses. Maw Maw wouldn't allow her to leave Joni alone, and she couldn't take her along.

"I want to watch TV." Poor Mikey. He had some sniffles and Dr. McCord didn't want him out in the rain no matter how warm it was.

"Get my bag, Sarah." Maw Maw had made Mrs. McCord a hot cup of tea when she came in from the rain. "Everyone sit down," she said. Maw Maw never spoke loudly, but when she spoke you listened. Maw Maw could have quieted a whole auditorium of kids. She could make them sit up, take notice, and behave!

"This is my storytelling bag." Sarah handed her a small deerskin bag that had been hanging in the room with the special things. "We have to be careful when we tell stories. If it's growing season, all the spirits that help things grow might stop their work to listen. But," she winked at Mikey, "I think the corn is doing well enough to listen to a story."

"We should be sitting around a fire." Chief Birdsong had walked into the room.

"Now, someone must pick something out of the bag."

Sarah smiled happily. "Whatever object you pick — Maw Maw has a story about it."

"Can I pick? Can I pick?" Naturally Mikey had his hand outstretched.

Maw Maw shook her head and smiled. "I think today we'll let Joni have the first turn. I know she's missing all her friends." For a minute Joni wondered whether Maw Maw knew about Raggedy Ann. She hadn't said anything. But Maw Maw had that way of looking into your heart, and she knew that Joni McCord was unhappy.

Joni tried not to be excited. She didn't want Sarah to think she was a baby. But she loved stories. Joni and Amanda used to make up all kinds of stories when they played together after school.

Joni closed her eyes and reached into the bag. She felt a few small objects, but her fingers seemed to close around something long and slender. She pulled out a tiny doll. It was made from a corn husk and dressed in a deerskin dress and tiny moccasins. She had long, shining black braids with a beaded headband. Everything was tiny but perfect.

"But the doll doesn't have a face!" said Mikey.

It was true. The face of the doll was empty — no eyes, ears, nose, or mouth!

Maw Maw took the doll, held it up for everyone to see, and began the story.

"Many moons ago in an Iroquois village not far from here, a beautiful baby girl was born. Word spread that she had the most beautiful black eyes and silky, long, black hair. Indians came from miles around just to look at her beauty.

"When she started to grow, she got prettier and prettier. Braves and warriors constantly told her how her eyes sparkled. She spent many hours combing her hair and tying and untying it with beads and ornaments. Her lips were red as strawberries and her cheeks reflected the sun's rays.

"Now, we all know that everyone in the village must share the work that is to be done. But not this maiden. She had been told she was beautiful so many times that she wouldn't do any work. Other girls helped their mothers cook, but this maiden just leaned over the kettle of water and stared at her reflection. 'I'm just too beautiful to cook,' she said.

"Some of the Indian maidens went to the river to wash clothes. But our beautiful maiden just leaned over the river and stared at her reflection, biting her lips to make them redder.

"One day as she stared at herself in the water, she heard a voice calling. She looked up and saw a rabbit. He hopped closer and said, 'I have been sent by the Creator to tell you to go back to your village and help your family.'

"But the beautiful maiden wouldn't listen. She was too busy staring at her reflection. A few more days passed and a bird in the tree called to her. 'Beautiful maiden, I have been sent by the Creator. This is your second warning. Your mother needs your help. Your younger brothers and sisters need watching. Return to the village and help them.'

"But she just sighed and leaned back over the riverbank to stare at herself.

"A day or two passed and then a week and the beautiful maiden still hadn't returned to her village. The chief gathered the villagers to form a search party.

"One small boy spoke up. 'She's down by the river, staring at her beautiful face in the water.' The villagers ran to the riverbank.

" 'I see her beaded moccasins,' cried the boy.

"All the villagers stopped and stared. The beautiful maiden was lying on her stomach. They could see her moccasins, her deerskin dress, and her beautiful black hair with the beaded ornaments. They turned her over and screamed in alarm. For the beautiful sparkling eyes, the strawberry lips, and smooth skin were all gone. The beautiful maiden had been turned into a corn husk. A dressed-up corn husk without a face.

"So, from that time on, all corn husk dolls are made without faces to remind children that just being beautiful isn't enough. You have to be good and kind, and help your family and your people, otherwise you will be remembered for being faceless!"

The room was quiet as Maw Maw laid the faceless corn husk doll on the table for everyone to look at once more.

"That was a good story," said Mikey. "Hey, Joni. You stare in the mirror at night when you comb your hair. Does that mean Joni's face will fall off, Maw Maw?"

"It's all right to look at yourself, Mikey. As long as you look and help other people around you, too."

"Wow. What else is in the bag?" He reached out with greedy fingers.

Maw Maw scooped it up quickly. "No more for tonight. We've got to eat and then get some sleep."

That night Joni dreamed of a corn husk doll. She was wearing a print dress and a silly, slightly dirty white apron. She didn't have a face, and instead of long black braids she had red hair made of yarn that stuck up all over her head.

Fifteen

The rain stopped. The sun shone through the loft window and woke the girls. Sarah had her head out the window first. She took a deep breath and sniffed the air. "Do you have a bathing suit?"

"Yes. I had two new ones I was going to wear to the town pool."

"That's right, the famous town pool. Do you think you can wear one to an Indian mud hole?"

Joni didn't know how to answer. Was Sarah teasing her again? In her letters she had told of a beautiful lake. How could you swim in a mud hole? She hopped out of bed. "Sure, I guess the suit can swim any place."

"Let's go."

Maw Maw fixed some corn bread and jam for

the girls and gave them a cold drink in a thermos. Mikey nagged to go along. "I need a big strong brave to help me in my garden. I was counting on you, Mikey," said Maw Maw.

Mikey wasn't sure. He looked at the girls and Maw Maw. He was wondering where he would have the most fun. "And I have an old hose to water those vegetables with. It seems to me that it's hot enough for a young man to wear his bathing suit while he waters."

"And no shoes?" squeaked Mikey.

"I think the shoes can stay off while you're watering."

"I'm staying," Mikey said.

The girls set off for the swimming hole. Again Sarah led Joni through backyards and cornfields and along country roads. Joni never saw any street signs or streetlights and knew she would never find her way back if they were out after dark. Sarah said hello to everyone they passed. Sometimes she would wave and sometimes she would stop and answer questions about her pa or Maw Maw.

"You know everyone and everyone knows you. In my town we only know the people on our block. Of course, people that bring their kids to my dad know him."

"The reservation is small and you have to be enrolled to live here. The land passes from family to family, so we know who belongs." Sarah paused. "We also know when strange cars drive through or when outsiders are around."

There it was again. Sarah always seemed to be reminding Joni that she didn't belong on the reservation. "Over there." Sarah pointed to a small hill with clumps of trees.

"I don't see any water."

"Follow me." Sarah ran to the top of the ridge. She threw down the food, her towel, and T-shirt and stepped out of her shorts. She disappeared down the other side of the ridge.

Joni followed. When she reached the top she could see why Sarah had hurried. This was no mud hole. It was a tiny lake fed by a bubbling mountain stream. Large trees grew along the bank, shading the edges, but the center of the lake sparkled so brightly that little wavy lines jumped up in front of Joni's eyes. A huge tree sat on the edge of the bank with strong limbs that grew out over the center of the lake. A long rope with a tire on the end was hanging from one of the largest limbs. Sarah was already seated on the tire swinging out over the water. "Can you swim? Watch this." And with a whoop she let go and splashed into the middle of the lake.

The tire kept swinging back and forth. Joni ran over and grabbed it as it came near the bank. "Is it really deep where you are?" Joni was just a beginning swimmer and she didn't like to be in water over her head. She was scared unless she could touch bottom. Besides, this was a lake in the middle of nowhere with no life preservers, lifeguards, or any grown-ups around.

"Sure, it's deep in the middle, but you can easily swim to the sides."

Joni sat on the tire and asked again. "Are you sure I'll be able to stand?"

"I thought you said you could swim." Sarah was treading water and she sounded as if she were getting annoyed with Joni.

Joni took a breath and tried to swing the tire out over the lake. She wouldn't let on how frightened she was of the deep water.

"Not like that," yelled Sarah. "Push off with your legs. Give yourself a running start."

"Like this?" Joni tried to push off. The tire barely swayed off the bank.

"Having trouble, paleface?" asked Oren Lodge. Joni had been concentrating so hard that she hadn't noticed him come down the ridge. She looked over her shoulders and saw the rest of Sarah's friends.

"We don't like strangers at our lake." There was Canada Shenandoah. She also saw Florrie Greeneyes and Nathan Mohawk at the top of the ridge.

"This is our special place," Florrie yelled to Joni.

Joni looked back to the lake. Sarah was still treading water. She hadn't said a thing. The Indian children had surrounded the tire and were holding it still. Joni swallowed hard as she looked into four pairs of dark, angry eyes.

"What do you think we should do with her?" asked Florrie.

"I know," said Nathan. "She wants to swing, so let's give her a swing." He and Oren gave the tire a big push. Joni held on for dear life. The tire swung over the water and then back to the lake bank. All four gave it another tremendous push. Joni felt as if her toes touched the sky before the tire swung back to the bank.

"Let go!" yelled Sarah. "Let go, Joni, and jump into the water."

The swing was going too fast. Joni was afraid to let go and she was afraid to hold on. They were pushing so hard she thought the tire might somersault in the air.

"Let go! Now!" Sarah yelled again and Joni closed her eyes and let go of the tire. The fall through the warm air was quick. She almost bellyflopped into the lake and she felt the cold sting of water on her thighs and arms. She forgot to hold her nose and down, down, down she went into the cold water. One toe hit the spongy bottom and, sputtering and flapping her arms, she quickly bobbed to the surface.

Oren grabbed hold of the tire, spun out over the lake, and, holding his knees, cannonballed right next to Joni. Florrie and Nathan followed until she was surrounded. Joni was still trying to catch her breath and tread water at the same time. She felt as if torpedoes were exploding on all sides of her.

"Help!" she screamed to Sarah. Oren, Florrie, and Nathan splashed Joni with huge sweeps of their hands and feet. "Help! I'm too far from shore to swim and I can't see."

The children kept laughing and splashing. Joni was beginning to panic. "I'm tired! I can't swim! Stop!"

She heard Sarah pushing her way through the splashing children.

"Help, Sarah, I can't tread water anymore. I'm too tired."

Sarah was yelling something. It was hard to hear her because the others were laughing so hard.

"Just put your feet down. You don't have to swim. You can stand," yelled Sarah.

Joni tried to stop treading water and put one foot down. She was so nervous that she didn't feel the bottom. Her head went under and she came up sputtering and spitting water. "Put both your feet down," yelled Sarah again.

Joni finally put her feet down. She felt her toes sinking into the squishy bottom. She stood up, ready to hold her breath again if she went under.

She stretched her body. She was standing. The water was only up to her chest.

The Indian kids were hysterical, laughing. Even Sarah. She pointed to Joni. "You should have seen yourself. You were so scared. You thought the water was over your head."

"Yes," yelled Canada. "You're such a baby. All you had to do was put your feet down and stand up."

They all collapsed in a heap of splashing water and laughter. Joni shook the wet hair out of her eyes and walked to shore. Even though the water had cooled her skin, she felt the heat of anger on her face. She was embarrassed and angry.

Embarrassed that they had played such a joke on her. She had been frightened on the tire swing and petrified that she was going to drown. But she was angry that Sarah had let them frighten her like this. They must have had it all planned. After all, it had been Sarah's idea to bring her here. Oren, Canada, and the others must have been hiding on the ridge just waiting to jump out at her.

She reached the shore and quickly put on her shorts and T-shirt. She didn't bother to lace up her sneakers. Just stuck her wet feet into them and started up the hill.

"Where are you going?" yelled Sarah.

Joni didn't answer. She didn't care if she got

lost. She wouldn't stay one minute longer around here. She was going to find her way to her father's clinic and talk to him privately. She could still feel some goo from the lake bottom between her toes. He'd have to listen now. Sarah and her friends had almost drowned her!

Sixteen

Maybe hunting and tracking and finding your way got into the blood. Even though she was angry and hurt, Joni managed to find the main road. She made a few wrong turns before winding up at the Medical Clinic.

Her hair had dried during her walk, and little curly ends sprung up around her face. She tried to smooth it down so she wouldn't look so wild. She grabbed a clump of grass and wiped the mud from her ankles and legs and tied her shoelaces. After she had tucked in her shirttail she walked into the clinic.

The waiting room was crowded with children and mothers. It was hot and noisy. There were jars on the registration counter. Instead of lollipops they were filled with fresh carrot sticks, celery stalks, and slices of cucumber. Dr. McCord didn't like to give little kids lollipops even when they got shots. He thought that all food, even snacks, should be healthy.

"Hi, honey." The door of a tiny cubicle opened and Dr. McCord came out. His stethoscope was twisted around his neck and he had a little Indian boy in his arms.

"Now, no more running for today, Calvin Kettle." Dr. McCord handed the little boy a carrot stick before he put him down. "You've got five stitches in that knee."

Calvin Kettle made a face. "I want a piece of candy."

Joni laughed even though she was impatient to get Dr. McCord alone. She knew how the little boy felt. She and Mikey always thought that candy tasted better than carrot sticks no matter how hard her father tried to convince them otherwise.

"Try this first, Calvin." Dr. McCord had the most soothing voice. Maw Maw's voice had the same sound. They could make snakes curl into little balls and wasps fold up their stingers.

"I need to talk to you, Daddy." Joni could feel the flow of tears starting.

"In a minute, hon." Two nurse's aides came up to Dr. McCord at once. "There's a phone call for you, Dr. McCord."

"Mrs. Jimerson has pains in her stomach."

"The Hoag boy has a bad headache again."

Joni felt like stamping her feet in frustration. There was an old saying. The shoemaker's children never had any shoes, because their dad never had time to make them a pair. He was too busy making shoes for the town. It was the same with doctors' kids. The doctors were so busy taking care of everyone else that they didn't notice when their own kids needed help.

"Wait inside by my desk, Joni."

Dr. McCord didn't have a big office like he did in New Jersey. There was just an old battered desk tucked behind a partition that had folding doors to give it some privacy. Joni picked up the picture that stood on the corner. It had been taken at the Jersey shore the summer before. She hated the way she looked. The sun had made her eyes all squinty. Her brother Alex looked big and tall and handsome. Joni wished that Alex were here. He would never have let those kids scare her like they did.

She realized there was a phone on her father's desk. Well, this wasn't like Maw Maw's rules. Joni didn't hesitate. She picked up the phone and dialed Mandy's number in New Jersey. She crossed her fingers as it rang and rang. Oh, no, don't tell me she's not home. The tears were starting again when she heard Mandy's giggle.

"Hello, it's me, Amanda Burnett, 222 Grand Court, Millburn, N.J., Planet Earth — if this is Hollywood calling, send the limousine — I'm all ready!" There was a lot of giggling on the New Jersey end.

Joni pictured Amanda's bedroom. She had a big canopied bed with pink flowered pillows and a comforter. There were white leather beanbag chairs to sink into and a pale pink and white couch. Amanda's mom even let her serve food in the room. Even crumbly refreshments like pretzels and stuff.

"Hi, Mandy?" Joni's voice was shaking.

"Sh. I can't hear." Mandy was trying to tell the other girls in her room to be quiet. "Who is this?"

"Mandy, it's me. It's Joni."

"Joni!" Mandy let out a shriek. "It's Joni!" She yelled to the immediate world. "Where are you?"

"I'm still here. Up here on the Indian reservation."

"Oh, I thought maybe you were home." Again Mandy stopped to repeat the information to the other girls.

"Who's there with you?"

"Oh, everyone. Courtney and Petey Mann and Sue — everyone. We were swimming at the pool and it started to rain. So my mom picked us up and we're in my room just hanging out."

Now Joni's tears really started. She wished for a magic carpet or maybe a tornado like Dorothy had in *The Wizard of Oz*. Anything that would whisk her off this reservation and into the cozy bedroom of her best friend.

111

"What's the matter?" Amanda asked. "You sound kind of funny." Before Joni could answer, Amanda had another question. "Courtney wants to know if you met any cute boys up there."

Cute boys! Joni tried to think if Oren and Nathan were cute. Maybe they were, but how could you like boys who practically tried to drown you?

Mandy asked if she had been swimming. Swimming! Joni still smelled the slightly stale odor the lake had left on her skin. She opened her mouth to tell Mandy what had happened. But she didn't know where to begin.

Dr. McCord's nurse, Ms. Deerpath, stuck her head in the door. "Sorry, Joni, your dad said to tell you that he has to set a broken leg. He's going to be a while."

Mandy was explaining that she had to hang up because her mom was going to take all the kids for pizza. Joni hung up the phone. She had never felt as alone as she did leaving the clinic and heading back to the Birdsong house.

Seventeen

Maw Maw could tell there was something wrong between Sarah and Joni. The two girls had changed and washed for supper but didn't look at each other. They were extra polite in front of the grown-ups. Sarah would say, "Please pass the rolls."

Joni would answer. "Here they are. May I have some butter?"

Maw Maw was explaining that the McCords would be able to be guests at the big powpow to be held at the Woodland Reservation. "You will just make it," said Chief Birdsong. "It takes place a few days before you go back to New Jersey. Indians will come from all over the country."

"There will be exhibits and booths and all kinds of food and Indian dancing." Maw Maw pointed to Sarah. "Sarah and her friends will take part in the dancing."

Sarah didn't look up from her plate. Ever since Joni had run from the lake, Sarah's stomach had felt like a colony of Mexican jumping beans. Sarah had followed Joni out of the lake and hid behind trees to make sure that Joni didn't get lost. When she saw Joni go into the clinic, Sarah went back home. One thing you could say for Joni, she thought. She isn't a squealer. Except for some sharp looks from Maw Maw, none of the adults said anything about today.

Joni was also aware that none of the adults knew the girls were angry at each other. Instead of being relieved, she was upset. Dr. McCord had been so tired that day when he walked in for dinner that he never even asked Joni why she had stopped by the clinic. And Mrs. McCord was just pleased that her library work was going well. Even though both her parents were working hard, Joni felt like they were taking a vacation from paying attention to her.

Chief Birdsong and Dr. McCord were having a discussion about the land that the Iroquois were living on. "Years ago," said the chief, "the Iroquois used to live on land from New England to the Mississippi River. Now we're cramped on fourteen reservations and whenever the government needs land, they take more from the reservation."

Mikey chimed in as he pushed the vegetables around his plate. "I know that Christopher Columbus found the Indians when he discovered America."

Sarah pushed back her plate. "How could Columbus find us? We weren't lost. We were living on our land and helped the white man or he never would have survived the winter."

Joni thought she would get a headache if the grown-ups started another discussion about the white man and the Indian. "Why are people still mad about things that happened so many years ago?"

Now it was the chief's turn to push his plate back. "Because, Joni, the white man has lied over and over again to the Indian. So we can't trust anymore. And there is no respect given for our ways, the traditional ways of the Indian."

Maw Maw spoke up in her quiet way. "Joni and Mikey are just trying to understand, and Dr. and Mrs. McCord are trying to help our people."

Sarah stood up. "Why do we always have to have outsiders helping us? We need our own doctors and our own librarians. But most times when our people get an education they leave, just like my mother."

Things got very quiet except for Mikey, scraping the sides of his plate as he tried to mash his potatoes. "The Indians gave us potatoes. I learned that when I was in school." He smiled at the chief. "But I wish you didn't give us tomatoes — I hate them — all red and squishy."

Even Sarah had to giggle at Mikey. "You like pizza, Mikey. Don't you?"

"Pizza? Yum!" His eyes lit up. "Are we going to have some for dessert?"

"Not tonight," said Mrs. McCord. "But the pizza you love has sauce that's made with squishy red tomatoes. So, no tomatoes — no sauce; no sauce — no pizza!"

"OK. Put tomatoes on the good list."

"I have to look through my special things for the Indian powwow. Who wants to help me?" asked Maw Maw.

"Me!" yelled Mikey.

Sarah had finished drying the dishes. "I'm going out for a while." She waited for Maw Maw to make her take Joni. But Maw Maw thought the girls probably needed a rest from each other. "Come along, Joni, you can help me pick out some things, too."

Maw Maw opened a small glass cabinet and took out tiny animal figures carved out of bone. "Careful." Mikey had grabbed for a small turtle.

"See these animals, Mikey?" Maw Maw held one in her hand. "The Iroquois people belong to clans. That means families that are related to each other. We have nine clans."

"And they're named after animals?" asked Joni.

"Yes," answered Maw Maw. "Named after Woodland animals. We have the hawk, turtle, wolf, bear, heron, snipe, beaver, elk, and the deer clan."

"What clan are you, Maw Maw?"

"I'm from the wolf clan."

"You're lucky. I'm just an ordinary McCord." Mikey looked sad; he thought that everything about the Indians was neat. "If you adopted me — would I be a wolf, too?"

"Absolutely," said Maw Maw. "As a matter of fact, we can give you an Indian name and adopt you into our clan."

Now Mikey looked a little nervous. "Does that mean I have to leave my Mommy and Daddy?"

"No. Not at all. We have to think of a special name for you. Then I give you a special string of wampum and we call it 'a name hung around the neck.' Which means it's your adopted name."

"That's neat. Let's do it. Please give me an Indian name."

"It's most important. We have to think carefully about what kind of person you are. We have to study the things you do."

"How about: 'he who forgets to wash up before bedtime'?" Mrs. McCord walked into the alcove. She had overheard the last part of the conversation.

"No!" wailed Mikey. "I don't want a name like that. Not hung around my neck."

117

Maw Maw laughed. "You go along with your mother, Mikey, and I'll think of an extra special name for you."

Maw Maw dug out some necklaces that had been strung with multicolored pieces of corn. She hung them around Joni's neck. "We'll have to have some more of these to sell at the powwow."

Joni picked up a belt that had pretty beading on it. Beading that looked familiar. She remembered Sarah's beaded bandanna. Maw Maw sighed as she took it out of Joni's hands. "Sarah's mother. She did the best work of anyone here. She had beautiful flower and animal designs."

"Doesn't she ever come back?" Joni asked.

"We never know when. She just shows up. Not to live here, of course, just to visit Sarah."

Maw Maw went through some papers tucked in a cubbyhole. She held up a card. "Actually it was her beading work that caused all the trouble." The card read: *Carlenia Birdsong, Authentic Native American Jewelry*. The address on the card was Washington, D.C.

"But I thought she left to go to college and be a social worker."

Maw Maw shook her head. "Is Sarah still telling that story? Carlenia sold jewelry to tourists from a tiny booth at the little store near the gas pumps. One day a lady came from a New York department store and wanted Carlenia to start a business.

Teach others on the reservation and sell lots of jewelry directly to the big stores."

"That sounds exciting. Is that what she did?"

Maw Maw looked very tired and her shoulders slumped. "No. My son wouldn't agree to it. He thought she would pick up too many of the white man's ways if she went into business. So she left the reservation and went into business anyway.

"Here's Sarah's dress. The one she'll wear for the powwow dances."

Maw Maw pointed to a pretty calico blouse and skirt. There were beaded belts and a necklace with a beaded wolf in the middle. Joni guessed that the wolf in the middle meant that Sarah was part of the wolf clan, too. "Her costume is so pretty."

"Not costume, Joni," Maw Maw said gently. "This is her traditional Indian dress. A costume is something you wear on Halloween. This is for our ceremonies."

Joni would try to remember that. But she couldn't help thinking that the Indian dress would make a super costume to wear in New Jersey for the annual Halloween parade.

Eighteen

By the time Joni was ready to go to bed, Sarah was in the room putting things away. Maw Maw had carried her Indian dress upstairs and Sarah was carefully hanging everything up.

For a few minutes the two girls didn't bother to talk to each other. Sarah took the beaded necklace with the wolf emblem and placed it carefully on one of her bookshelves. "My mother made this," she said to Joni.

Joni couldn't believe it. Was Sarah just going to pretend that nothing had happened today? Sarah only talked nicely when her friends weren't around. When they appeared, she tried to make Joni disappear! I'll just ignore her, thought Joni, as she opened a book and pretended to read.

Sarah kept talking. "I got a card from my

mother. She wants me to visit her in Washington later this summer. She even sent me the plane fare. I've never been on a plane before."

It was no use. Joni was reading the same sentence over and over again. Besides, what Sarah was saying was more interesting than her book. "You've never been on a plane? Ever?"

Sarah slammed a drawer. "Oh, I forgot who I was talking to. I'm sure Joni McCord, Miss America, has flown all over the world. Of course, I'm just a poor Indian — "

"Wait a minute!" said Joni. "I wasn't trying to put you down. And I haven't been all over the world, just to Florida by airplane. And once to my uncle's wedding in Chicago."

Sarah was quiet for a while. "Did you see my headdress?" She held up a beautiful beaded headband that tied with pieces of deerskin. Fancy beadwork was woven in and out of the strips of deerskin and hung down the sides.

"Maw Maw showed me most of your things."

"My mother made this, too."

"I know. She really does great work." Somehow Joni didn't trust Sarah being friendly.

"For a while she was happy on the reservation. She was making jewelry and selling it."

Joni bit her tongue. She had to pretend that Maw Maw hadn't already told her the true story of how Carlenia Birdsong had left the reservation.

"I told you that she's going to college in Washington. But that's not true. She's really in Washington making and selling jewelry."

"But that's neat. You must be proud of her."

"I would be — but Pa . . ." Sarah's voice trailed off. Joni felt sad for her even though she had been so mean. It was like Sarah was stuck between two worlds. She was proud that she was an Iroquois and she knew all about her heritage and culture from Maw Maw and Chief Birdsong. She even knew her language, which was more than a lot of Indian kids did. But living on the reservation meant she was cut off from her mom.

"So, are you going to go to Washington?"

"I don't know. Maw Maw said I should go and Pa said I'm old enough to make up my own mind. But even though he acts tough I think he's afraid for me to go. Maybe he thinks I'll be like my mother. Say I'm going for a visit and never come back."

Joni felt a lump in her throat. What if she had to choose between her own mother and father? That would just be too hard. But at least both of them lived in the same world. Not like Sarah's parents.

She tried to change the subject. "Maw Maw told Mikey and me about the clans today." Joni pointed to the wolf in the middle of Sarah's necklace. "But you wear a turtle necklace, too."

"This one." Sarah held up her small turtle with the turquoise and coral chips on his back. "My mom made this, too. It's because the Iroquois called North America, 'Great Turtle Island.'"

"How come?" asked Joni, touching the turtle.

Sarah hesitated. "You'll make fun."

"OK, so don't tell me."

"Well. It's really a good story. When my mother sells a piece of jewelry she writes out the story that goes with it. This way the person learns a little bit about our traditions."

That sounded good to Joni. So good, in fact, that she wondered why Chief Birdsong would object.

Sarah sat at the edge of her bed and dangled the turtle by his silver chain. "There was once a world way up in the sky where people something like humans lived. And underneath this sky world there was no land, just a great big sea. One day a sky woman asked her husband to uproot a great tree. He did and left a big hole in the sky. The woman wanted to look through it to see the world below. As she was looking, she slipped and fell through the hole.

"The water animals were watching and they sent a large bird up to catch the sky woman before she landed in the sea. Then a giant snapping turtle offered his back to support the sky woman. The other animals wanted to help and make sure she had lots of room to walk around on. So they dove

123

to the bottom of the sea and brought up mud and piled it on the turtle's back.

"The sky woman kept walking in a big circle and the land grew and grew on the turtle's back. And that's how North America came to be called Great Turtle Island."

By the time Sarah finished the story it was dark in the room. Joni lit the lamp. "I'm glad you told me. When I go home, I'm going to tell all my friends. Especially Amanda. She has these two pet turtles at home. They have flowers painted on their backs and she keeps them in a big glass jar."

"Pet turtles?"

"She's allergic to dogs and cats. Turtles are about the only things that don't make her sneeze. She'll like the story."

"Here." Sarah rummaged in a drawer and brought out a thin, printed sheet of paper. "It's a copy of the story written down."

"Oh, thanks." Joni took the piece of parchment paper and smoothed it out.

"Wait a minute." Sarah opened a shoe box that was under her desk. It was filled with all kinds of animal shapes. "Here's one for you." She handed Joni a small turtle that was almost identical to her turtle necklace, except it didn't have any colored stones on its silver back. "Something to remember me by."

"Thanks!" Joni couldn't believe how nice Sarah

was acting. She put the turtle necklace around her neck.

"Want to see how this would look on you?" Sarah asked, twirling her beaded headband in her hand.

"You'd let me try it on?"

"Sure." The girls went over to the mirror and Sarah pushed the bangs off Joni's face and tied the headband around her forehead. It felt heavy at first because of all the beadwork. "This is really great," Joni said. "I feel just like Pocahontas."

"You don't have to make fun." Sarah's voice changed and she whipped the headband away.

"What did I say now?"

"You don't get it, do you?"

"No! First you're nice. Then you get mad."

"Ever since I was a little girl, when people find out I'm Indian they say, 'Oh, what a cute little squaw,' or, 'How is Pocahontas?' As if every Indian girl was named Pocahontas. I thought you would realize that, just from living on the reservation with us."

"But I didn't mean to insult you. Pocahontas is the only Indian name I know."

"No, it isn't. My name is Sarah. Why couldn't you say you feel or look just like Sarah?"

"That's it!" Now it was Joni who turned her back and tossed her head in anger. "I'm not speaking to you anymore. No matter what I say it seems to be the wrong thing. You tell me people always pick on Indians. Well, you've done nothing but pick, pick, pick at me since I got here. And today your friends tried to drown me and you didn't do anything about it. You probably told them you were bringing me to the lake so they could do it!"

Joni paused for a breath. She took off the small silver turtle necklace. "And here's your Great Turtle Island necklace back. I don't want anything from you."

She heard Sarah giggle. "It's insulting to give a gift back to the giver."

"I don't care. No matter what I do, you think it's insulting."

Sarah's giggles turned into belly laughs. Joni tried to ignore it but the laughter got louder. She turned around to face the young Indian girl. "I don't see what's so funny."

"Not now. But this morning, at the lake, you looked so funny when you were splashing around trying to tread water — when all you had to do was put your feet down and walk away." Sarah laughed so hard she rolled over on her side and hugged her pillow.

Joni tried to keep a stern face, but Sarah's laughter was catching — just like the measles. "I guess I must have looked pretty funny, but you told me that the middle of the lake was deep. And I told you that I didn't swim too well."

"That's for sure. But you didn't tell me you couldn't *walk* in water, either." This time Joni's giggles spilled loose also. Sarah turned the light out, but for the next hour, the moonlight shone on two girls wrapped in matching patchwork quilts whose shoulders moved up and down with laughter.

Nineteen

"Come on, Joni Bird Legs, get up." Joni groaned as Sarah pulled the covers off.

"What time is it?" Joni put the pillow over her head to keep out the sunshine.

"It's morning, and I have to do an errand for Maw Maw, so get up."

After a quick breakfast Joni found herself on the main road with Sarah. "Where are we going? Not to the lake again, I hope."

"No. I've got to pick some things up for Maw Maw in town."

"Town?" Joni looked around. All she saw were the huge overgrown trees and the cornfields. "Where's the town?"

"Right outside the reservation."

Joni pictured her hometown of Millburn with

Main Street lined with stores, places to eat, and a twin movie theater. The girls passed the Longhouse. No one was around. "Pa is having a meeting at his trailer. The state wants to build a dam and wants to use reservation land."

"What's the dam for?" asked Joni.

"More electrical power for the factories. You would think they have enough electricity. Our lake and a bunch of houses around it would be gobbled up by the dam."

The lake where you almost drowned me, thought Joni, but she didn't say anything. "Can't your pa just say no, that you don't want to sell? After all, he's the chief."

"All the chiefs from the reservations around here are going to meet at the powwow. It won't do any good. How are we going to fight the whole United States government? Use all the tomahawks and bows and arrows that old women like Maw Maw have hanging on their walls? The Bureau of Indian Affairs in Washington will have some meetings with the chiefs and then decide how much money the land is worth and every member of the reservation will get some."

"That's good, isn't it?" asked Joni. "At least they pay you for the land."

"Sure. But where are we going to live if they keep taking our land back piece by piece? That's one reason my mother wanted to leave. She thinks

129

we can live off the reservation and still keep our customs and traditions. Pa says that'll be the end of us as a separate nation."

Joni hadn't been off reservation land since the McCords had arrived. The girls came to the end of the unpaved road. There was a small sign that marked the reservation, and they stepped onto smooth, paved roads. There was a gas station and a large, all-purpose variety store.

"This is the town. We go in there." Sarah pointed to the store and took out her list. "These are some things Maw Maw needs to get ready for the powwow. Things they forgot to get at the big mall." Sarah grabbed Joni's arm as they walked into the store.

"What's the matter?" asked Joni.

"Nothing." But Sarah put her head down and buried it in her list. There were three or four kids standing around the aisles. They didn't look like they were from the reservation. They blocked the aisle as Sarah tried to pass.

"Well, look who's here. Our little Indian squaw; did someone let you off the reservation?"

Sarah took a deep breath. "Get out of my way, Charlie Miller."

"Hey, hey, the Indian girl's got a temper. Going to get your braves to scalp me?"

Sarah motioned to Joni. "Don't pay attention to them. They're in my school."

"That's right. It was a really good school until they let all you Indians in."

Sarah's face flushed as she tried to go about collecting the things on her list. The three kids followed her up and down the aisle, teasing and taunting.

Joni wondered why the clerk by the cash register didn't stop them. Charlie Miller turned to Joni. "What are you doing up here? You don't look like an Indian."

"That's right," said another. "But if you hang around with them, the color red will rub off on you."

They seemed to find this hysterically funny and laughed all over each other. Finally the clerk walked down the aisle. "What's going on down here? What's all the commotion about?"

Joni waited for him to throw the kids out of the store. They were surrounding Sarah, who had her arms full. "Hey you, Indian girl. Why are you causing all this trouble? Come on, get out of here. I'm not in the mood for trouble today."

"Wait a minute!" Joni almost choked on the words. "Sarah wasn't doing anything but shopping when these other kids started in on her."

"Quiet, Joni," said Sarah.

The clerk turned to Joni. "Oh, and who are you? Another Indian from the reservation? Then you're out of here also. Go ahead — get out!"

131

"Better search them, Tony. I think the Indian was trying to steal some stuff," said Charlie Miller. Joni gasped at such a downright lie.

Sarah put the things in her arms down on the counter as if she knew what was coming. "Empty your pockets, too," said the clerk. He turned to Joni. "You, too; empty your pockets."

Joni wanted to protest. They had done nothing. This was the United States of America, and you had to have proof before you accused someone. But she closed her mouth when she saw the hostile and laughing faces. Joni and Sarah pulled their pockets inside out.

"OK. You can go," said the clerk. "Do you want to pay for these things now or do you have more shopping to do?"

Joni waited for Sarah to tell him to stuff it, but Sarah gathered up the items and waited by the register. After she paid, the two girls left the store.

"Why did you pay? How could you buy those things from him after he was so horrible to you?" Joni barely waited until the door shut behind them before she started to yell at Sarah.

"Right. Except you forgot that Maw Maw needs these things. This is the closest store unless you want her to drive sixty-five miles to the mall for thumbtacks. This is the way people who live near the reservation treat Indians. They treat us like dirt, because they know no one cares about us anyway."

"But I don't understand — " Sarah didn't let Joni say any more.

"That's right you don't understand, white girl, so just shut up and mind your own business." And Sarah ran past the reservation sign into the woods, leaving Joni to stare after her.

By the time Joni reached the Birdsong house Sarah had been there, dropped off the shopping bags, and left. Maw Maw studied Joni's face. She knew there had been trouble again but she wisely remained silent, waiting until one of the girls felt like talking about it.

Dr. McCord had taken half a day off to go fishing with Chief Birdsong. The table was set for lunch. No one said anything about Sarah, so apparently they weren't expecting her to eat. Joni began to realize that Sarah treated her *on* the reservation the way people treated Sarah *off* the reservation. But it wasn't fair. Joni wasn't the same as all those others.

She tried to follow the conversation. Chief Birdsong was worried about the dam. He had to hold meetings about that and at the same time organize the powwow. Since Sarah's pa was chief of the Woodland Reservation, he was supposed to receive wampum belts from the museum to officially open the powwow. The chief was angry that the belts were kept in museums. "They belong to us," he said. "How would you like it if your sacred objects were in a museum?"

133

Dr. McCord didn't have an answer. Another touchy subject brought up at mealtime. Dr. McCord would have to treat them all for indigestion if this kept up. Usually Joni didn't pay too much attention to the table talk, but after what had happened that morning, she kept her ears open.

"Can I wear a wampum belt?" asked Mikey. Everyone at the table broke into laughter. You could always count on Mikey to break the tension. When he said something silly it was considered "cute." If Joni said it, Sarah wouldn't talk to her for hours.

"Wampum belts aren't belts you wear to hold your pants up, Mikey," Chief Birdsong said.

"True wampum beads are made from round clam shells, purple or white. Our ancestors would string them on pieces of twisted elm bark," said Maw Maw.

"When a treaty was signed, the white people would write it down. But the Indians kept a record of the treaties by writing it into a pattern on the belts.

"Messages were sent back and forth by wampum belts, Mikey," Maw Maw continued.

"If one chief wanted to go to war he'd make a red wampum belt. If another tribe accepted the belt, it meant they would join the war. If another tribe threw the belt on the ground, it meant they wouldn't go to war." Chief Birdsong took a deep breath.

Joni now understood how Sarah knew so much about her people and their customs. She got lessons every day, all day long. Chief Birdsong thumped the table so hard the glasses jumped. "So you can see why we're angry that our wampum belts are in museums, locked behind glass doors, and not with the tribes that can appreciate them and read them. All our history is in those belts."

Mikey copied the table thump by banging with his fists. He wasn't strong enough to make the glasses jump. "Let's go get the wampum belts out of the museum."

"It isn't as easy as that." But Chief Birdsong laughed. "I'm sorry if I got so angry that I spoiled your meal," he said.

Joni finished her sandwich slowly. That morning she had gotten a taste of how prejudiced people could be toward Indians. Sarah had to face that every day, plus listen to her father deal with all the problems on the reservation. No wonder Sarah felt like she couldn't trust Joni.

Joni took a deep breath. Now that she understood things a little better she would try harder to make friends with Sarah.

After helping Maw Maw clean up, Joni climbed the ladder to the loft room. The room was quiet and empty without Sarah. It was warm, too, with the sun shining on her pillow. Her eyes closed and she fell asleep.

Joni dreamed about wampum belts with all kinds of messages on them. In her dream the clerk in the convenience store kept screaming that she was a thief. Sarah arrived holding some belts. "They're bright red," Sarah said. "War belts. We're at war with all you outsiders."

"But I'm on your side," Joni said. It was no use. In her dream the belts kept wrapping themselves around her neck and she woke up choking. Only it wasn't wampum belts that were choking her, but the tangle of the quilt that had twisted around her neck.

Twenty

Joni awoke hot and sweaty from her nap. She wondered what time it was. The sun was starting to go down and the house was quiet. She had slept the afternoon away. That was one thing about summer on the reservation. Everyone had things to do, and they might or might not get together at mealtime. Sarah hadn't returned. She was probably with her friends. After what happened that morning it was no telling when she'd get back, or what kind of a mood she'd be in.

After she washed, Joni went downstairs. All of a sudden a noise cut through the heavy air from the backyard. Sarah had arrived with her friends, everyone but Nathan Mohawk. There were other groups, young Iroquois that Joni hadn't met yet. Some of them looked older, as if they were in high school. They were all dressed in traditional clothes. The girls wore long full skirts with colorful overblouses and leggings made of deerskin. They had belts and necklaces with the clan emblems and all kinds of headdresses. Some were very simple and others fancier. Sarah's pieces had the best beadwork. Joni took notice and she felt proud, almost as if the two girls were really part of one family.

The boys were also wearing leggings and overblouses. They had bells on the bottoms of their pants that jingled as they walked. Joni saw Oren Lodge walk over to Sarah. He looked taller in his native dress and had a proud look on his face.

Two of the bigger boys began to play the water drums. The drums made you want to tap your feet. Joni opened the living room window and leaned out so she could get a better view. Maw Maw had a water drum in her collection, so Joni had seen one but never heard it played. The drum had a round bottom and was covered with stretched deerskin. There was a small opening to pour water in. Like putting gas in a car. Then the drummer would turn the drum upside down and soak the deerskin top. The wet skin made an extra thumping sound when it was played, almost like an echo. When the deerskin dried out, the drummer would just tip the drum upside down to soak it again.

The musicians used special rattles that were carved pieces of wood with dried seeds inside. The players shook them in time to the drums, and they had a nice rhythm.

Joni realized this must be a practice session for the powwow. The dancers had formed a big circle, as if they were around a bonfire. Joni stretched farther over the windowsill. Her elbow hit a potted geranium. The plant landed with a crash that made all the dancers turn around. She quickly pulled her head back in the window — heart beating hard. But not before she heard Canada Shenandoah. "It's that girl. She's spying on us."

There were some grumbles from the group. Joni heard Sarah's voice. "Let's go behind my pa's trailer. The ground's flat and *no one* will bother us!"

The group moved and soon Joni could hear the sound of drums and rattles, only much more softly, coming from behind the trailer. Joni made her way back upstairs. There was nothing to do until dinnertime. She'd write a letter to Amanda. At least time was passing and pretty soon she'd be back in New Jersey.

Joni reached for the carton near her bed where she kept her personal things. There was a breeze stirring through the large tree outside the window. Branches were tapping against the glass. Something caught her eye. Joni dropped the box and opened the window wider. There was a rope hanging from one of the branches. It swung back and forth just out of her reach. Something very familiar was tied to the end of the rope. This was no Indian warrior face with green eyes and feathers. And this was *no* dream. Joni saw red yarn hair, a button eye, and a dirty white apron covering a print dress. Raggedy Ann.

Joni grabbed a wire hanger from the room and stretched as far as she could out the window. She hooked the rope with the hanger and pulled it slowly into the room. It was extra slow going because the rag doll would catch on sharp branches that were sticking up. Finally Joni had her old friend in her hands. But there was nothing to hold. The doll had been slit from the head all the way through the body. All the stuffing was gone. Joni leaned out the window again and saw a pile of soft feathers that had been the insides of Raggedy Ann. Even the arms and legs had been slit open and the feathers that were left inside now loosened and flew around the bedroom.

Joni tried to hug the doll anyway. Raggedy Ann didn't even smell the same. Her hair had grease smudges, and there were grass stains all over her clothes. She smelled like she had been stored in a chicken coop. Joni tried to smooth Raggedy Ann's yarn hair. Her stomach was in a tight ball. This was it. Joni had had enough. Sarah Birdsong had been nasty since the day Joni arrived on the reservation. The scary face in the tree the very first day. Stealing Raggedy Ann, practically drowning Joni in the lake, and now returning Raggedy Ann all cut up and ruined. Sarah always knew where Joni was, and that was how she planned these things. Sarah couldn't wait a month for Joni to leave. She kept trying to push her out. Well, fine! Joni was steaming now. She wasn't even scared anymore, just hurt and angry. If Sarah wanted war, she would have it. Joni wrapped the ruined doll in an old T-shirt and placed it in the bottom of her duffel bag. Maybe when she got back to New Jersey her grandma could put it together for her. Right now she wasn't going to let Sarah Birdsong see how upset she was. Joni McCord was on the warpath. She just wished she had a red wampum belt to throw at Sarah.

"Hi, how come the window's open so wide?" Sarah had quietly come up the ladder and crossed the room to the window. She closed it halfway and turned the lamp on. Probably trying to see if I found the doll yet, thought Joni.

"Oh, I'm tired." Sarah flopped down on her bed. "We were practicing dancing all afternoon. The girls' dresses are downstairs; Maw Maw is going to make sure there aren't any tears."

Sarah didn't seem to notice that Joni wasn't talking. "Everyone's really excited about the powwow. I wrote my mother." Sarah hesitated. "Maybe she'll come. She could have a booth for her jewelry. People always buy lots at a festival." She sat up and looked at Joni. "Are you all right?

You're awfully quiet. Maybe Maw Maw can make you some chamomile tea — Indian medicine. It'll make you feel better."

Joni couldn't stand it anymore. She went to the duffel and took out her T-shirt with the doll inside. She unwrapped it and threw it at Sarah.

"Hey, watch out! What is this?" Sarah tried to duck the flying object.

The Raggedy Ann landed on the floor. "What's this?" Sarah bent down. "This looks like your doll." She started to giggle. "Wow, she looks like she was run over by a locomotive. What happened?"

Joni pulled the doll back out of Sarah's hands. "Sure. Very funny. Play dumb. Nice and dumb like a good little Indian." For a minute Joni caught her breath. She shouldn't have called Sarah a dumb Indian.

Sarah was on her feet. "What are you talking about? And who are you calling dumb?"

"This is my stupid doll, remember? You told me to get lost and take my doll with me. But you couldn't wait, could you? You had to keep scaring me and then take my doll and ruin it. Sometimes you act friendly and then, before I know it, you're mad. I can take that. But why did you have to punish me for coming up — ?"

Now Sarah interrupted. "I knew from your dumb letters that you never wanted to come up here. You're just like all the other outsiders. My

142

friends and my pa are right." Sarah opened drawers and threw some clothes in an old backpack. "Stay here, paleface. I'm going to Pa's trailer. And when you're gone I'll have a special ceremony to purify my room."

Sarah climbed down the ladder, backpack over her shoulder. Joni followed behind. "Sure, go ahead. Act all innocent. Go to your father's trailer. Who cares? I can't wait to get out of here and go back to New Jersey."

It was lucky that the house was empty. Sarah slammed the front door so hard that the floor shook under Joni's feet. And the screams that the two girls had hurled at each other like stones hung in the air of the quiet room.

Twenty-one

"Sarah is staying with her father in the trailer for a few days. She thinks she's coming down with a cold," Maw Maw said at dinner.

Dr. McCord spoke up. "Would you like me to look at her?"

Maw Maw spoke quietly, her eyes on Joni the whole time. "No. She'll be fine. She just needs some rest before the powwow. The lake was probably too cold to swim in."

It was hard for Joni to get to sleep. She was used to hearing Sarah breathe and toss and turn next to her. The moonlight rested on the empty pillow. Sarah had been so angry, and she had acted so innocent. Could it be some mistake? But no, who else could have done all these things?

* * *

Joni was groggy in the morning. Again it seemed as if everyone had something to do but her. Mikey was helping Maw Maw with the powwow and Dr. McCord was at the clinic. Mrs. McCord was helping to organize a booth that would show special historical books telling the history of the Iroquois.

Joni wandered outside. It was a beautiful day. The sun was hot but there was a breeze blowing. She looked at the sky. There weren't a lot of wires around to mess up the trees like there were in New Jersey, and she didn't see any smokestacks or chimneys to make smog. Sarah had told her that Indians were the guardians of the earth. The white people had polluted the air, ruined the lakes and the ocean, and destroyed forests.

Joni walked to the side of the house where the big elm stretched up to the loft window. She looked up at the branches. Maybe she had just dreamed that Raggedy Ann had been hanging from there. No, she bent to the ground. It wasn't a dream. There on the ground, drifting between the roots of the tree, were the soiled feathers that had been the doll's stuffing.

Joni felt mad and angry and very, very hurt. She looked over at the trailer. There was no sign of Sarah. She went back into the house. A clothes rack stood in the living room holding the Indian dresses. She fingered them gently. There was Sarah's. It was the prettiest, because of all the

145

beadwork her mother had done. There was the necklace with the wolf clan emblem in the middle. It was looped over the hanger. Joni thought about the night Sarah had let her try on the headband. Then she remembered how angry Sarah would get for no reason at all.

One of Raggedy's feathers must have caught on her sneaker. It was loose now and flew in Joni's face on a gust of air. Joni swatted at the feather, her anger rising again. She reached for the wolf clan necklace and slipped it off the hanger without thinking. She heard the door slam and the voices of Mikey and Maw Maw. Joni stuffed the necklace under her loose sweatshirt before they walked into the room.

"Hi." She walked quickly past Maw Maw. "I was just going down to the library to help my mother." Joni held her hands across her stomach so no one would see the bulge. Once outside the house she stopped to figure out what to do next. She thought of Sarah going to the clothes rack and searching all over for the clan necklace. Good! She would know how it felt to have something important missing. It would serve Sarah right if the necklace were ripped apart, the same as Raggedy Ann.

Joni walked across the open field. No. It was better to have Sarah go through the powwow wondering where the necklace was. Then at the end of the day, Joni would let her find it. Or maybe

Joni would take it back to New Jersey and wait for a year and then mail it back. Or maybe. . . .

Joni's mind was working overtime, trying to think of the plan that would hurt Sarah the most. She looked around for a rock or tree trunk, a place where the necklace would be safe, yet hidden.

Joni found herself near the small tarpaper store where she and Sarah had gotten soda. There were a lot of voices. One even sounded like Sarah's. That was one of the troubles at Woodland Reservation. It was so small that sooner or later you ran into people whether you wanted to or not. Besides, this was a hangout for Sarah's friends. Joni tightened her grip on the necklace. The sharp beaded corners were sticking into her stomach. She certainly didn't want Sarah or her friends to find her with the necklace now.

It was Sarah. Joni ducked behind some large holly bushes. No one saw her. Sarah was yelling at Oren, Florrie, and Canada. Nathan Mohawk was trying to slink away. "Get back here, Nathan! Answer me; who stole that stupid doll and who ripped it up?"

"We all did it, Sarah," said Florrie. "OK, Nathan climbed the tree to steal it, but we all planned it."

"Remember when you read her letters to us?" Canada asked. "None of us wanted her up here. You didn't, either. She's one of them and can go

147

anyplace she wants. Her family didn't have to come to the reservation."

"Right," said Oren. "We treated her the way white kids treat us off the reservation."

"What about that green-eyed face she saw the first day? I thought she was making it up to get attention," Sarah said.

"Wasn't that neat?" Florrie giggled. "We painted a balloon, got some helium from the gas station, and made a headdress from chicken feathers. Oren made the green eyes. He copied mine because he said the white girl would be scared of a green-eyed Indian."

"I climbed up early in the morning and tied it to a tree limb," said Nathan, proudly pounding his chest.

Sarah folded her arms. "How did you happen to appear at the lake? Canada, you knew I was going to take her swimming. I even asked you to go along. But you said you had to help your mother."

"I know. I told the guys and we thought we'd scare her away but good when we got her in the lake. And it almost worked, too."

Oren doubled over in laughter. "You have to admit it was pretty funny watching her tread water."

Nathan agreed. "Outsiders always think the worst about us anyway. She really believed we were going to drown her. I thought for sure she'd go back to New Jersey after that."

Sarah stamped her foot. "Well, it wasn't funny when you stole her doll. First I thought she had hid it herself to get me in trouble. Then I realized it had to be you guys. I should have gotten it back right away, but I thought you were playing a joke. That you'd keep it for a while and then put it back."

Joni felt her cheeks burning as she listened. It didn't make sense. Sarah kept asking her friends how everything had happened. If Sarah didn't know, that meant she hadn't been part of it.

Now Sarah's friends were racing each other to tell her everything. They had planned to put the doll back on the bed but thought they could get rid of Joni before the powwow if they ripped it up. They knew what had happened to Sarah at the general store. They had all been taunted different times off the reservation. Joni would pay for all those insults.

Nathan Mohawk had left the dancing practice to climb the tree and leave the doll hanging. He peeked in the bedroom first to make sure that it was empty. The tree was so thick he couldn't be seen from other parts of the house.

"But why are you mad at *us*?" asked Canada. "Why should you care about this girl?"

Joni was still listening. She heard Sarah's next words loud and clear. "Because Joni McCord was an invited guest in my house. She ate with us and slept with us. You made me break Indian hospitality, and I'm shamed and so is my pa. Even though I didn't know what was going on, I didn't protect her in my own house."

"Oh, Sarah. Come on. Don't be like that," said Florrie and Canada almost in a chorus.

"We don't want you mad at us," Oren chimed in.

"No," said Nathan. "It's that girl's fault. She doesn't belong on our reservation."

Joni didn't wait to hear any more. As the Indians walked into the little store she turned to run back to the house. Her heart was pounding. Sarah hadn't had anything to do with all the bad things that had happened! Oh, what terrible things Joni had said to Sarah! She felt sick to her stomach. All the conversations at the Birdsong dinner table, about how the Indians felt they could never trust the white man. Joni had proved that to Sarah by accusing her without any proof, never thinking it could have been someone else.

Joni cut across the road, trying to decide whether to go to the library or to her father's clinic. She took the necklace from underneath her shirt and held it as tightly as she could. The wolf in the center looked as if he were blinking at her. *Go*, he seemed to be saying. Be as fast and as cunning as the wolf. Joni jumped a small wooden fence and came to one of the cornfields. She cut across it, trying to get her bearings. Yes. The clinic was over to the right.

Joni zigzagged through the dried cornstalks. She had to get to her father. He'd tell her what to do, and how to apologize to Sarah. There was a low strip of barbed wire around a lettuce patch. She jumped the wire and kept running. When she hit the main road again, she slowed down to catch her breath. Joni felt a pain in her right leg. It was bleeding. She had cut it jumping over the barbed wire. Joni didn't care. As long as she hadn't dropped the wolf necklace. Oh, no! She noticed that some of the beads holding the wolf onto the chain were coming apart. Maybe it had happened when she held it under her shirt. Or maybe she had clutched it too hard while running across the fields. Sarah wouldn't be able to wear it. The whole necklace would come apart when she started to dance.

Joni was out of breath and her leg hurt. She sat down in the field. She was hot and sweaty. She tried to smooth the necklace. She couldn't fix it. All those delicate little beads strung together. It started to rain. Joni looked up at the sky. Maybe it would be a big storm and the powwow would be canceled. She only saw two dark clouds in the sky but both of them were right over her head!

Twenty-two

Joni walked the rest of the way to Dr. McCord's clinic. Ms. Deerpath, his nurse, spotted the blood on her leg. "Joni, what did you do to yourself?"

Joni was afraid the nurse would tell Dr. McCord that she had been crying. But Joni was so wet and bedraggled from the rain that Ms. Deerpath didn't notice the tears. She made Joni sit on one of the examining tables and started cleaning the cut on her leg. For once it was quiet at the clinic, probably because of the storm. Dr. McCord came in and gave Joni a hug. She started to cry when she felt her father's arms go around her. "Joni, how did you do this?" He took over from Ms. Deerpath. "It looks pretty deep. I think you're going to need stitches. What did you cut it on?"

Joni's dad was all doctor now. He sounded the way he did when he was taking care of any patient. Joni told him about the barbed wire. Dr. McCord raised an eyebrow. "I didn't know you were training for the Olympics." Dr. McCord knew Joni wasn't a great athlete who would go jogging through fields and over fences.

"She's had a tetanus shot this year, so we don't have to worry about that," he told Ms. Deerpath. The nurse placed a needle and some sutures on a steel tray.

"Is this going to hurt?" Joni asked.

Dr. McCord had never stitched Joni before. Like most doctors he didn't like to take care of family in case he did have to hurt them.

Dr. McCord gave Joni a shot of novocaine and five stitches. She bit her bottom lip so she wouldn't cry out. "Hold still," said Dr. McCord. "Another minute, Joni, and I'll be finished."

Ms. Deerpath had noticed the necklace that Joni was clutching in her hand. "Let me take that from you, Joni, so you can lie back and relax."

"No." She held it to her chest, not willing to let it out of her sight. Dr. McCord noticed the tears streaming down his daughter's cheeks. "I'm all finished, Joni. It shouldn't hurt anymore." Dr. McCord rubbed the back of his neck. "Any more carrot sticks left, Ms. Deerpath?"

"I don't think so, Dr. McCord."

"Tell you what. This calls for stronger stuff, anyway. Two cherry lollipops, Ms. Deerpath. I'll have one, too."

Joni was still crying and it wasn't because of her leg. She thought there must have been a hole in her head, too. What else would make her take Sarah's necklace? Too bad her father hadn't been around to take some stitches before her brains leaked out.

"Let me see what you've got there, Joni." Dr. McCord gently pulled the necklace out of her hands. She was too tired to fight. "The wolf clan," he said. "Does this belong to Maw Maw?"

"No. It's Sarah's." Joni couldn't hold back any longer. The whole story came tumbling out. The face in the tree, the lake, the return of Raggedy Ann, and how she thought Sarah was responsible for everything. Joni knew her father would be disappointed when she told him how she had taken the necklace, and he was.

She waited for him to yell and scream; that would make her feel better. But Dr. McCord just shook his head and sighed. "Here your mom and I thought you and Sarah were getting along. We especially hoped that living with these good people would help you understand their problems."

Joni felt lower than an ant. "Well, let's see what we can do about Sarah's necklace. Maybe we can patch this up. Then we'll see about patching up the people problems." Dr. McCord spread the necklace on the examining table and looked for the spots where it was starting to loosen.

"Daddy, I know you mean well, but the beads

are so tiny, you can barely see where they're stitched together. Sarah's mother must have used invisible thread."

"I just stitched you up, didn't I?" Dr. McCord asked.

"Yes. But that's different, Daddy."

"Different? I've put tiny stitches inside people and outside, so when they heal not even the smallest scar shows. Stand back."

Joni moved aside. Ms. Deerpath brought the doctor some white silk sutures and the thinnest needle. She turned on the overhead light. It looked as if they were operating. Dr. McCord put on special glasses that had little magnifiers at the end. It would have looked like a real operation if he had put rubber gloves on.

"Hold it still, Ms. Deerpath."

"Yes, Doctor."

They talked to each other softly and Ms. Deerpath held onto the necklace firmly while he stitched. About fifteen minutes later he stood up. "I think we've got it." He stretched his neck and Ms. Deerpath handed Joni the necklace.

It looked perfect. She turned it right side up and upside down and every which way. She couldn't see where Dr. McCord had put in the new stitches. It wasn't the slightest bit loose. As a matter of fact he had even tightened the clasp that held the piece together.

"Oh, Daddy." Joni threw herself in his arms.

155

Dr. McCord gave her a big hug. "Now let me check *your* stitches once more, young lady." Her stitches were perfect, too. "Wait for me in the car, and we'll drive home together."

Joni limped to the car. OK. The necklace was fixed. Now she had to get it back on the hanger before Sarah noticed it was missing. Joni and her father talked things over on the way to the Birdsong home. "You owe Sarah an apology, Joni. For blaming her for all those things that weren't her fault."

"But why didn't she say something when they were happening? Why didn't she tell me she didn't have anything to do with it?"

"If she thought her friends were responsible she was probably trying to protect them. At least until she had proof. Which was more than you did. You were a guest in her house, in her room, and you didn't trust her."

Joni squirmed in the car. There was nothing Dr. McCord could say that would make her feel worse than she already did.

Sarah wasn't in the house. Mrs. McCord made a big fuss over Joni's stitches. Mikey just wanted to know if she had gotten a lollipop.

"Yes," she answered. "A red one."

"No fair."

Dr. McCord pulled a yellow pop out of his pocket and rumpled Mikey's hair. He hated the children to eat sweets except on special occasions. Right now he didn't want Mikey banging his leg up to get equal attention.

The necklace was wrapped in some cotton and covered with plastic wrap. Joni tried to get into the living room to put it back with Sarah's dress. She finally got away from the adults by pretending to go to the bathroom. Her heart fell and she couldn't breathe. The clothes rack was gone and so were all the Indian dresses.

She sat down for supper. "Is Sarah coming for dinner?" she asked.

"I don't think so." Maw Maw shook her head. "I think she and her pa have things to do this evening."

Maw Maw gave Joni a plate full of fried corn bread. There were big piles already wrapped for tomorrow's powwow. Usually she loved it, but the lump in her throat wouldn't let her swallow right. All this attention was making her feel more miserable. If Maw Maw and her mother knew everything that had happened today, Joni would be the last one getting fussed over.

Joni's leg was starting to throb so she climbed the ladder to her bedroom. She put the necklace on the floor underneath her bed so no harm would come to it.

Mrs. McCord climbed the ladder, bringing a cool glass of a delicious strawberry drink. That was also specially made for the next day's powwow. She sat at the edge of the bed and smoothed

Joni's hair back. "Poor Sarah's had a bad day also."

Joni's heart couldn't sink any lower. Her mom didn't know how bad Sarah's day had been. If Dr. McCord hadn't fixed the necklace . . . Joni shuddered.

"A package came for Sarah from her mother. Maw Maw had written Mrs. Birdsong about the powwow, hoping that she'd come back for it."

"Is she coming?"

"No. She sent a large box with some beautiful jewelry in it, to be sold at a booth."

Joni could imagine how Sarah felt. She wanted her mother and instead she got a cardboard box. Mrs. McCord's hands felt so cool on Joni's forehead. You almost didn't need stitches when you had a mother around to patch you together.

"Was Sarah upset?" asked Joni.

"I'm sure she was, but you know Sarah. She hides her feelings. She has so much pride. She wouldn't want anyone to know how badly she feels. She just picked up her costume and went back to the trailer."

Joni knew. Sarah would never cry, at least not in public. Instead she'd get terribly angry when she was feeling hurt.

Mikey climbed halfway up the ladder. "Mom, Joni, come see what I helped Maw Maw with. Come see! Quickly!"

Joni hobbled down the ladder after her mother. Outside, Chief Birdsong was loading large wooden

158

crates to take over to the powwow. "See." Mikey pointed to the foods inside the crates. "It shows all the Indian foods that the colonists learned about. Maw Maw made little signs for them. We got most from the garden and the hills in the back."

There were apples and wild cherries, peaches, plums, grapes, all kinds of berries: blackberries, raspberries, blueberries, huckleberries, strawberries, and cranberries. The ones that didn't grow at that time of year had been dried in Maw Maw's root cellar and were neatly labeled. There were all kinds of corn and beans, green beans, purple lima beans, wild peas and squashes and pumpkins and melons. Mikey pointed to his favorite — not for eating but the most fun picking: the wild mushrooms and puffballs that grew around tree roots. The mushrooms made Mrs. McCord nervous because she was afraid Mikey would pick something poisonous and eat it.

"And I'm going to stand at the booth tomorrow, Maw Maw said so. And I'm going to tell everyone about all the food. I know what they are even if I can't read all the signs."

Maw Maw came out of the house. "I think," she said to Chief Birdsong, "that we finally have a 'name to hang around the neck' of this adopted Iroquois."

"What," said Mikey. "Quick, tell me."

Maw Maw closed her eyes and placed a single

strand of wampum beads around Mikey's neck. "Laughing Boy Who Brings Help and Friendship."

"Oh." Mikey's face fell for a minute. "Can't I be Fastest Runner or Warrior?"

"There are plenty of young braves who can run fast, Mikey," said Maw Maw, "but not many who bring help and friendship."

He didn't seem convinced. "Well, OK, I guess."

"How about if we make it, 'Fastest Laughing Boy Who Brings Help and Friendship,'" said Chief Birdsong.

"That's good. I like that."

"OK, Fastest Laughing Boy," said Mrs. Mc-Cord. "I think it's time you washed up. You look like you made fruit salad with your bare hands."

Joni watched the chief drive off. The wheels of his truck kicked up some mud from the unpaved road. Joni was glad that Maw Maw wasn't giving her an adopted Iroquois name. The only name she had earned was that of "Biggest Ratfink"!

Twenty-three

Joni had never been inside the Birdsong trailer even though it was on the lot next to the house. She hadn't been invited and you didn't barge into homes on the reservation.

It was obvious that Sarah wasn't going to come to the house for any meals, and Joni wanted to bring her the necklace. Dinner dragged on and on. Joni could hardly eat. No one bugged her because they thought her leg was hurting. The grown-ups were going over to the powwow grounds after dinner. There were things to set up and get ready. The wrapped necklace was still under Joni's bed.

Maw Maw bustled around gathering more things from her treasure room. "It's going to be a beautiful day tomorrow," she said. "I can tell. Mother Earth is going to be good to us."

Maw Maw was always aware of the sky and the earth, and all the beauties of nature. But right now Maw Maw was worried about her granddaughter and the young girl from New Jersey. Sarah had run over for a sandwich, making sure Joni was nowhere in sight. She insisted that nothing was wrong. She just wanted to stay in the trailer until the powwow was over and the McCords were on their way back to New Jersey.

Maw Maw studied Joni. Maybe she would be the first to open up. "I noticed all through dinner that something is bothering you. Something more than your leg." She didn't want to scare Joni away but she could tell that the girl needed to talk.

Joni sighed. It was no use keeping things from Maw Maw. She had that ability to see right through a person, and maybe she could help. Joni had to get that necklace back to Sarah before tomorrow. So she told her story for the second time that day. Everything that had happened between her and Sarah since the McCords had arrived at the reservation.

Maw Maw didn't say anything when Joni finished. For a minute Joni wasn't sure she had heard the worst. "I have her necklace, the wolf clan piece, the one her mother made. Maybe she knows it's missing already."

"Sarah knows," said Maw Maw. "She and her friends were searching the field behind the trailer all afternoon. She thought she might have lost it during dance practice."

"What should I do?" Joni asked. She had to get the necklace back to Sarah before the powwow began.

Maw Maw put her arms around Joni's trembling shoulders. "Let's go out to the garden." Joni wondered why on earth they were going to the vegetable garden, but she was too desperate to question.

Most of the vegetables and fruit were already picked, but there were a couple of corn mounds left, planted in the traditional way. "See." Maw Maw ran her hands over the silk tassels on top of the corn. "In the olden days, our ancestors counted on three main plants to live: corn, beans, and squash. They were called the three sisters, for it was believed that each plant has a female spirit. The three sisters or spirits dress themselves in the leaves of the plant to protect the fields."

Joni reached down to one of the ears of corn. She didn't know what corn, squash, and beans had to do with making up with Sarah, but she listened anyway.

Maw Maw continued. "The Indian way is to grow the corn, beans, and squash together in one mound. We don't put them in separate rows. They use the same soil and they don't hurt each other. The corn doesn't take too much water away from

163

the squash and the beans don't take too much sun away from the corn. Yet, when they grow and ripen they still remain true to themselves. The corn doesn't turn into beans and the squash doesn't turn into corn. They're three sisters sharing the same earth but growing up peacefully and in harmony."

Joni stared at the cornstalk. It seemed as if Maw Maw was telling her that she and Sarah were like the three sisters. They should be able to share the earth and the sky without fighting over it. Yet they didn't have to become exactly the same. They could grow up with the things that made them different and interesting like the corn, the beans, and the squash.

It made sense. It wasn't just her and Sarah. All people should be able to share the land without ruining it for each other. People could be different, like the three sisters, but still get along.

But how could you make this happen? Joni realized that she and Sarah would have to learn more about each other and learn to trust. But you couldn't very well learn to trust someone if you weren't talking to each other!

Again, it seemed as if Maw Maw were reading Joni's mind. "You'll think of a way," she said. "Everything cannot be done at once. Just as there is a growing season, it takes time for trust to grow also."

"But what should I do?"

Maw Maw just smiled. "Put your feet down solid on Mother Earth. Look around at the rocks and trees that have been here always. Feel and listen to the breeze and watch the moon that has laughed at how silly man has been. They'll help you think."

Maw Maw went back in the house. Joni lifted her face to the sky. She felt the breeze playing with her hair, and watched the moon shine down on the three sisters.

Twenty-four

Joni went back into the house and got Sarah's necklace. "Where are you going?" asked Mikey. There was a note telling Joni to stay with Mikey since all the adults had gone back to the powwow grounds. He was doing a puzzle at the kitchen table. "I'm going to tell Mom that you're going out of the house and leaving me alone."

"I thought you were the Fastest Laughing Boy. Do you want it changed to Fastest Whiner?" asked Joni. "I'll be back in a minute."

It was so quiet with everyone gone. Joni walked toward the trailer. Maybe Sarah had gone with them. She took a deep breath and looked up at the moon again. She couldn't let Sarah go through a sleepless night, worrying about her necklace even if she never spoke to Joni again.

There was no buzzer or bell on the trailer, just some wooden wind chimes that were strung from a flagpole. They moved as she walked past. Joni had to bang on the screen door. She could see a small light under the door. But what if Sarah was already sleeping? The days were long on the reservation, and people went to sleep early.

The door opened. Sarah was still dressed. Her eyes were red and swollen. Joni knew it wasn't allergies that made them look like that. A lot of tears must have been shed.

"Sarah?" Joni couldn't see into the room because Sarah was blocking the way.

"What do you want?" Sarah's voice was hoarse, the way a voice gets when you do a lot of heavy crying.

"Can I come in for a minute?" Sarah hesitated and looked over her shoulder. At first Joni thought someone was in there with her. Then she realized that Sarah might be embarrassed to have her come in.

"I just wanted to give you something."

Sarah opened the door and stood aside. "It's just an old trailer," she said.

There was an electric wire that had been strung from the main house to the trailer to supply electricity. There were wooden bunk beds covered with colorful woven blankets. An old porcelain sink was in the corner, and next to it was a big jug of bottled water. There was a tiny chipped refrigerator and a couple of chairs. Some pictures of Indians in old-fashioned clothes hung on the wall. It was clean and neat but very small and shabby.

"There's no TV here, either, if that's what you came to see."

"No. I got used to no TV at Maw Maw's house."

"Now when you go back to New Jersey you can tell your friends about the Birdsongs' broken-down trailer."

This was going to be harder than Joni thought. "Sarah, I have to tell you something." There was no easy way to say it. "Here's your necklace!" Joni handed over the plastic-wrapped bundle.

Sarah opened it quickly. "Oh, it's back!" Her whole face smiled. "Thanks, Joni." Sarah put it over her neck and held onto the wolf's head in the center. "This was one of the first things my mother made me. It's really my good-luck piece. I was going crazy all afternoon. You really are nice. Where did you find it, in the house? Outside?"

Joni gritted her teeth. It would be so easy to leave now, and Sarah would never have to know. But Dr. McCord and Maw Maw knew the truth. She couldn't lie to Sarah and then try to be friends. "Sarah." Joni tried to speak as fast as possible. She kept her eyes on the floor so she wouldn't have to look at Sarah's face. "Sarah. I thought you took my Raggedy Ann and ripped it up. I even

168

thought you planned for your friends to scare me at the lake."

Sarah interrupted. "I knew that. The minute anything happened I could tell you thought I had done it."

"I know. I was wrong and stupid. I was so angry when I found Raggedy Ann ripped up that I took your necklace."

"You *took* it!" Sarah stepped backward, as if she were trying to get away from a rattlesnake.

"I know. It was like I was crazy and wanted to get back at you. I wouldn't have ruined it or anything. I tried to put it right back but I had to have stitches in my leg and then the dress rack was gone. I was going to give it to you before the dancing began."

Sarah wasn't listening. "I told you all about my mother. You knew she made this for me. You're just like all the rest of the people who treat Indians like dirt."

"No, I'm not. Really, Sarah. I know you don't believe me. It was just so confusing coming up here. Sometimes you'd act friendly, and then you'd be mad — "

"But I never took anything of yours or did any damage to you. I tried to stop my friends. They were just trying to protect me from you."

"That's another thing. Sometimes you'd make plans with me, and then you'd go off with your friends and not invite me."

"I was trying to convince them you were different from other outside kids. But you're worse. Sat at my dinner table and ate Maw Maw's food and then stole my necklace."

"Sarah!"

Sarah opened the door. "Get out of here. Oh, don't worry. I'll dance tomorrow and I won't tell my friends that you took the necklace. When Indians give their word on something they keep it. Besides, I wouldn't ruin the powwow or upset Pa; he's got too much to do already."

"Sarah, can't we" — the door slammed shut in Joni's face — "be friends?" She saw the light go out in the trailer. It was quiet except for the mournful jangle of the wind chimes.

Twenty-five

Joni tossed all night. Mikey yelled up the stairs in the morning. "It's powwow. Powwow! Let's go!"

Joni groaned as she got out of bed. Her head felt like it was full of feathers but her legs were so tired they felt like fifty-pound weights. She stuck her tongue out at the mirror. Maybe she had a temperature, and she could go back to bed under the covers and stay there until the powwow was over, the McCords all packed, and on their way back to New Jersey.

"You look very tired, Joni. Maybe Daddy better have another look at that leg," Joni's mother said.

"No. It's all right, Mom."

Maw Maw handed Joni a cup. "Drink up. Time for Indian medicine. Elderberry tea. It'll make you feel better. I had to mix some for Sarah this morning. She looked as bad as you." That was all Maw

171

Maw said, but she knew something had gone on between the two girls the night before and it wasn't good.

Joni felt the warmth of the tea through the pottery mug. She didn't have much time left to make a new start on the reservation. Maybe she and Sarah couldn't be best friends; they had gotten too messed up. But it wasn't too late to trust again. Maw Maw had said it last night. Not only corn, beans, and squash needed time to grow. So did people.

The powwow grounds were crowded. People had come from all over. Indians from other reservations in the United States and Canada were milling around. A lot of them wore native dress. The booths were crowded with people buying Indian arts and crafts.

The food booths were popular, too. Everyone seemed to be munching something delicious-looking. Wooden bleacher seats had been borrowed from the local high school and set up in the field where the dancing was going to take place. Wood was stacked in the center, ready for a huge bonfire. There would be dancing and storytelling around the fire until late in the night. The booths would be open all day.

Joni had Mikey by the hand. "I'll take Mikey over to the bleachers so we can save good seats," she said to her parents. They were helping Maw

Maw at one of the booths. A small sign stated ORIGINAL AND TRADITIONAL NATIVE AMERICAN JEWELRY BY CARLENIA BIRDSONG. Necklaces, rings, bracelets, and earrings were spread on a woven piece of cloth that had been placed over the rough wooden table boards.

Joni and Mikey sat in the middle of the bleachers. She saved seats for her mother and father. Joni spotted the young dancers arriving at one end of the field. They were in their native dress. Maw Maw was there tying ribbons and straightening headpieces. Joni spotted Sarah, who had her arms folded and was talking to Canada and Florrie Greeneyes. The wolf clan necklace glittered in the sun. There were a dozen drummers and rattle shakers who were lined up in a semicircle around the bonfire.

The stands were filling up. Joni looked for her parents. Some rough-looking town kids carrying beer cans sat in the stands above Joni and Mikey. They were loud and noisy. One of the boys was sprinkling popcorn on people seated below him. Right now everyone was good-natured, but it was only a matter of time before the boy would annoy people and start a fight.

The dancers moved out and formed a circle around the bonfire. Chief Birdsong held up his hand for quiet. The bleachers were jammed and latecomers stood around the field. Some had brought their own folding beach chairs to set up.

The chief had all his ceremonial clothes on. Even his eagle headdress. "Wow," said Mikey. "He looks just like the movies. Only better. And we know him." Mikey turned to the couple in back of them. "That's Chief Birdsong. We live in his house." Mikey waved his wampum string. "See, the chief even adopted me."

Joni was embarrassed and tried to shush him, but the people were interested and one lady even asked to see his wampum string. Chief Birdsong stood so still and straight and strong, he almost looked like a statue. He was so dignified, the stands quickly quieted out of respect. Joni felt a warmth in her chest. "I live there, too," she said to the couple.

"What an experience," said the lady. "You're lucky children." Joni smiled. She wouldn't have thought so a month ago, but now . . . if only Sarah would talk to her.

The chief welcomed everyone to the powwow. He thanked all the volunteers for their hard work. In a sudden move he held his arm straight out like a piece of steel and pointed to the drummers. Joni nudged Mikey to watch as the water drums were tipped to wet the deerskin coverings. The rattle shakers began to play.

First the dancers did a welcome dance. The drumbeat excited every one, and the bleachers began to shake as the visitors moved their feet. Some of the elders joined the circle of young dan-

174

cers singing and chanting to the ancient rhythm. The sound curled up and mingled with the smoke from the fire. One of the dancers explained each dance before it began.

There was a competition dance or snake dance where the dancers tried to outdo each other as they danced around the fire. The bonfire was going strong. The air was crisp for a summer's day and the clean smell of smoke was all around. The dancers got a lot of applause each time they finished.

The Native Americans who lived on the reservation were beaming. They were so proud. They were entertaining as a nation on their own piece of land. Even if it was small, it was theirs. They were in charge and they wanted all the visitors to have a wonderful time.

Mikey loved it. He stood on the bleacher seat and bounced up and down in time to the music. Joni closed her eyes and listened to the chanting and felt the vibrations of the drumbeat through her feet. With the smell of the fire in her nose she tried to think of what it must have been like hundreds of years before when the Indians owned all this land and lived on it, and hunted and farmed and fished for their families. When the trees weren't poisoned with acid rain. When the air wasn't polluted from all the factories.

The rough kids in the stands started to get louder. They were making all kinds of cracks

175

about Indians and a beer can landed near the dancing circle. The grown-ups around them told them to shut up or leave.

The dancers did a rabbit dance, which represented the rabbit being chased through the woods. After that the dancers announced a traditional friendship dance.

The Indian dancers again began in a circle. But the circle changed to a straight line and the chanters seemed to be calling for people to join in the back of the line. Joni watched Indians from the sidelines, even those dressed in regular clothes, fall in at the back of the dancers. The drums were getting louder and louder.

"Why don't we go dance?" asked Mikey. "All those other people are." More and more people from the sidelines and stands were joining the friendship dance. It didn't seem as if you had to know the exact steps. People kind of bounced along to the drumbeat.

"I think this dance is just for Native Americans, Mikey," Joni whispered. "I don't think any outsiders are joining in."

"It's a friendship dance, isn't it?"

Joni watched Sarah whirl around in the line. She seemed to be going faster and faster to the drums. "Hey, look at all the squaws out there. Any scalps for sale?" The boys in the stand were getting rough again. Joni saw Sarah glance up at the noise. She saw the tension in Sarah's face as she wondered if white people were going to spoil the powwow like they had spoiled everything else.

Joni's eyes were caught by some waving corn in the fields across from the powwow grounds. The three sisters! "Stay here, Mikey," she said as she made her way down the bleachers to the dancers.

Twenty-six

Joni got on the end of the line of dancers, in back of Florrie Greeneyes. She tried to follow Florrie's steps. There were hoots from the sidelines. Florrie turned around and saw Joni. Her mouth opened and she stopped dancing. She stopped so suddenly that Joni almost crashed into her. As soon as the other Indian dancers saw Joni, they stopped dancing also.

Joni tried to ignore them all and keep dancing. But it was hard. Oren spotted her. "Hey," he yelled. "What are you doing? This is an Indian dance." He stopped dancing and pulled Canada and Nathan Mohawk to the sidelines next to him. Sarah looked up, saw Joni, and stopped whirling. She stared at Joni, who kept moving, dancing, turning, and hopping. Sarah moved out of the circle to stand with her friends. The chanters and

178

the drummers stopped playing. People in the bleachers stood up to see what was happening.

The last drum stopped. It was dead quiet. Just the crackle from the bonfire and the murmurs from the dancers who were giving Joni dirty looks. She was the only one still moving. The murmurs were louder. "This is supposed to be an Indian dance."

"Who does she think she is?"

People were yelling from the bleachers also. "Hey, girl, get out of there and let the Indians finish their dance."

All the dancers had backed away from Joni. It was as if she had a terrible disease. Joni looked at the sky. There were no answers up there. Oh, please, she prayed. Let there be an earthquake or a hurricane or a flood or let the ground open up and swallow me whole, or let me wake up and be in my bed in New Jersey and have this whole thing be a dream.

But no, there was Joni McCord in the middle of a silent but angry circle of Indians. Out of the corner of her eye she saw Dr. and Mrs. McCord and Maw Maw running across the field. She finally stopped dancing and stood still. Her heart was pounding, and her face was red-hot. It wasn't from the bonfire. Joni was afraid she had started another war with the Indians.

"But it's supposed to be a friendship dance!" Mikey's clear voice rang out across the field. Nobody moved. Joni looked for a way to slink back into the crowd.

Suddenly Sarah stepped back to the bonfire next to Joni. "You sure are one crazy girl," she said. But Sarah didn't look angry anymore. She took Joni's hand. "Dig your feet into the ground and feel the earth as you dance. And listen to the drum; it's like your heartbeat. Let it move you around."

Joni tried to follow Sarah. It was hard since there were no drums. But she wasn't alone anymore. Now there were two crazy kids whirling around the bonfire. Chief Birdsong walked over to the drummers. Joni's heart dropped. She knew how he felt about tradition. She and Sarah would probably be carried off the field together, or maybe thrown into the bonfire.

The iron arm pointed and the drummers started up again. Slowly at first, then the rattlers and the chanters joined in. Joni closed her eyes. Sarah was right. She felt the drums as if they were her heartbeat. They sent her whirling around and around. When Joni opened her eyes she was surprised to see that the other dancers had returned. The drums got stronger and stronger, and more people rejoined the dance.

Then something strange happened. People began to leave the bleachers to join in the line of friendship dancers. Indians, non-Indians, kids, and old people. The rough kids were still hooting and hollering in the stands, but no one was paying any attention to them.

"Guess what?" Sarah had to yell over the drums. "I'm going to visit my mother in Washington."

"Neat. So you'll get your first airplane ride," Joni said.

"Nope." Sarah twirled around, and Joni had to lean closer to hear. "Pa has to go to Washington to the Bureau of Indian Affairs, and he's going to drive me. He promised to stay and visit after his meetings."

"Wow." Joni danced in place. "It's a long ride to Washington, and you have to pass right through New Jersey to get there," she shouted to Sarah.

Sarah just smiled and shrugged her shoulders. Mikey ran out to the field and grabbed hands. Sarah and Joni lifted him in the air as they twirled around. Dr. and Mrs. McCord had joined the group and they took Mikey between them.

The drums had gotten into Joni's blood. She wasn't even tired. She could have danced forever. Sarah slipped her wolf clan necklace off and spun closer to Joni. As the girls turned, Sarah placed it around Joni's neck. The glow from the flames reflected off the wolf's eyes and he seemed to wink at the girls.

The line of dancers held hands as they wove their way around the fire. Sarah's hand closed tightly around Joni's slender fingers. Joni felt a tap on her shoulder. She turned and looked into a pair of beautiful green eyes. "Can I squeeze in here?" asked Florrie Greeneyes. "Sure," answered a smiling Sarah as she made room.

Joni reached for Florrie's hand. Florrie's fingers closed over Joni's. Suddenly Canada was in front of them, hopping to the beat as she tried to keep up with the moving circle. "You were my friend first," she shouted to Sarah.

"I'm still your friend. Now get in the circle, you silly thing," Sarah said as she made a space for Canada.

That's just the way Amanda and I act when we're afraid someone else is coming between us, thought Joni. She realized for the first time since coming to the reservation that Canada and Florrie Greeneyes must have been jealous that she was staying in Sarah's house.

The drummers weren't a bit tired. The rhythm got faster and faster. There were so many dancers on the field that another circle was started, led by Oren and Nathan Mohawk. "We don't dance with girls," shouted Oren as he and Nathan danced past the girls.

"Who cares?" shouted Sarah, and she rolled her eyes at Joni as if to say, Aren't boys silly? Joni laughed out loud. It was true. Boys could be so silly, and the two Indians boys were no different than Petey Mann when he acted up.

Across the moving circles of happy dancers Joni saw Maw Maw. She stood still and dignified, her arms folded across her chest, hair shining in the fading rays of the sun. She thought Maw Maw was smiling right at her. As she watched, Maw Maw raised her hand and pointed to the cornfields that surrounded the powwow grounds.

The silky tassels of the cornstalks were waving in the breeze. They seemed to bend and sway in time with the drums. Joni smiled back at Maw Maw. She understood. For today at least it was peaceful on the Woodland Reservation. The children were happy and so were the three sisters.